KICKIN' SASS

C.D. GORRI

KICKIN' SASS

Dire Wolf Mates 4
by C.D. Gorri
Edited by BookNookNuts

Edited by BookNookNuts

For Lori and Tammy,
Thank you for always cheering me on, and for your
unwavering support.
Xoxo, C.D.

Before you begin sign up for my newsletter here:
SUBSCRIBE HERE

BLURB

Summer fun meets eternal love in this sass kickin' fated mates romance!

Phoenix Tala is taking a break from his new home on the border of Blue Valley where his Pack and MC have recently settled down.

With his Dire Wolf feeling out of sorts, he takes a road trip to clear his beast's mind. But the Fates have more in store for him than an easy ride.

Tracey Donner is tired of her upper-crust parents' disapproval. After a shopping trip gets nasty, she takes off for the one place she felt happy as a child. Maccon City, New Jersey. She is ready for some serious changes in her life. But until then, a girl could have a little fun, couldn't she?

Of course, she never expected to run into that fun face first.

Literally.

A spontaneous moonlight skinny dip turns into something else when she swims into a midnight bather with more muscles than she knew was possible for one man to have.

Willing to dive into a vacation fling with the bad boy biker, Tracey is all about the moment, but Phoenix has forever on his mind.

Can he convince the luscious female to be his mate?

PROLOGUE

The smell of fire filled her nostrils and young Tracey gasped as the air grew thick with it. She hid under the bed, scared of what was happening. Mother had called her naughty again and Tracey was so ashamed.

She had embarrassed her mother in front of her friends again, but she didn't mean to. The fancy women were all dressed up and sitting outside on the enormous stone patio beneath the bright yellow awning Father had ordered specifically for Mother's tea parties.

Tracey had only wanted to join in the fun. She put on her best Spring dress, but she'd only just come home from boarding school, and it was from last year. It was too tight and squeezed the chubby parts of her belly and arms, but she had to look just right.

Mother would never approve of her wearing her school clothes to a party. So, she squeezed herself inside of the uncomfortable outfit and slathered some of her mother's blush and lipstick on her face.

She looked grown up now, for sure. Maybe Mother would finally smile at her the way other children's parents smiled at them when they were proud or happy. Tracey knew if she could just make her mother proud, she would like her more.

"What are you doing, you naughty girl?!" Mother had screeched when she spied Tracey standing proudly in the doorway in her too tight dress and borrowed heels.

"I wanted to surprise you—"

"Go to your room right now, Tracey Donner. Wash your face and burn that dress. I have never been so embarrassed," she'd snapped, pulling Tracey by the elbow into the hallway.

Burn the dress?

But it was the only one she had. Tracey's lip quivered, and she shook. Her mother's brilliant blue eyes flashed like lightning, and tendrils of fear snaked up her spine.

"I never should have let your father talk me into allowing you to come back here," Mother snarled.

"I'm sorry," she whispered.

"Yes, Tracey, that is what you are. Sorry and pathetic. That is all you will ever be."

Tracey did not understand the reason for her mother's cruelty, but that night, something new had happened. That night, Tracey stopped trying to win her mother's affection and approval. That night, she became angry for the first time in her young life.

But while she was coming to grips with her anger, an accident happened. A small fire broke out during her mother's tea party and that beautiful yellow awning father had ordered special burned to ashes.

Smoke wafted into the house, up the stairs, and to Tracey's room, making it difficult to breathe. She waited there for what seemed like hours after the sirens had come and gone, nevertheless, no one came looking for her.

She heard Mother and Father talking downstairs. Her parents rarely argued, but they seemed in the middle of a big one now. They were discussing her school and her time home, and misery the likes of which she'd never known filled her. Mother wanted her gone, but Father seemed against it—and still, she waited.

No one came to check on her, and she'd yet to move from her hiding spot. Her stomach was rumbling by the time the sound of unfamiliar footsteps climbing the stairs reached her ears. This was it. The moment some driver her parents hired came to take her back to the boarding school she hated.

Tracey stifled her scream with a hand over her mouth. But the simple sneaker-clad feet stopped in front of her bed. A woman kneeled down, her wide smile easing some of the hurt Tracey was feeling.

"*Hola, linda,*" she spoke softly.

"Hi," was Tracey's shy response.

"My name is Rosa, and your parents just hired me to take care of you. Would that be alright?"

Tracey's tiny heart pounded inside her chest.

"You're coming to school with me?" she asked curiously.

"No, I am too big for school. You will take the bus with the other kids, but I will be here when you get back. We are going to be great friends, *si?*"

Tracey nodded. For the first time in her life, she had a friend.

CHAPTER 1

The department store reeked of expensive perfume samples and cosmetics. Between that and the heat outside, it was positively stifling.

Still, the overpowering fragrances should have stopped bothering Tracey now that she'd moved on, but they were still making their way through her olfactory senses. Her allergies were the very devil. Easily influenced by minor changes in her environment—*and these were not minor.*

For Pete's sake, they must have used a thousand civets to make one stinking bottle!

Tracey had tried to dodge the pushy women trying to sell the bottle of high end French perfume at $350 an ounce, but she got her with two generous squirts. It was all Tracey could do not to sneeze all over her.

Luckily, there was a tissue box nearby. Her mother was not at all amused. Really, she should have been better prepared, but who knew you needed tactical defense lessons before visiting a mall?

Oh well.

She'd smiled apologetically, grabbed a second tissue, and followed her mother, whose patented glare was boring holes into Tracey's head. She was there for one reason only, and that was to assist her mother with whatever she needed. Apparently, checking out the newest summer arrivals in the shoe department was a necessity.

After forty-eight minutes and thirty-three seconds of browsing and watching her mother try on one pair of painful looking heels after another, Tracey was more than ready to call it a day. Shopping was sheer torture with the woman. Why had she ever agreed to go?

Because you still want Mommy's approval.

Pathetic? Probably. But Tracey had always wanted to be closer to her mother. If she could just figure out what it was exactly the woman didn't like, maybe she could fix it and they would both be happier.

"Tracey? Are you listening to me? Hand me the other pair. These must be irregularly sized," Daniella Donner—first lady of the upper crust community of Rumson, New Jersey, and Tracey's mother, made a tsking noise as she removed the ridiculously expensive sandal from her freshly pedicured foot.

"Sorry, I was just thinking," Tracey murmured and moved to grab the next box from the ever-growing pile of uber high-heeled, strappy, pointed toe, rhinestone studded, and grossly uncomfortable footwear.

It was a shame, really. There were plenty of trendy shoes out there—orthopedics, recommended by her podiatrist—that would definitely be a better choice for her mother. But Tracey kept her lips zipped, knowing she would never even consider it.

No matter how tight the older woman tried to hold on to her youth, some things were inarguable. Such as the fact her mother's foot had grown a size and a half over the years, starting immediately after she'd become pregnant with Tracey some thirty years ago.

Not that she'd admit it. To hear her tell it, Tracey

might as well be an alien. She looked nothing like either of her beautiful parents.

Not only was she what her mother called *unpleasantly plump,* but her coloring was all wrong. Comfortable in her size sixteen Levi's, Tracey might have too many curves for her petite stature, but she was fine with that. It was the fact she stood a whopping five feet three inches tall compared to her elegantly thin five foot eight inch tall mother, and her six foot tall father, that was so dang disappointing. But hardly her fault.

As if that was not bad enough, Tracey also lacked the trademark crystal clear, sapphire blue eyes of both her parents, Daniella and Daniel Donner—*the Donners* of Rumson. Though, admittedly, her father's eyes were a few shades darker than his wife's.

Good thing or she'd have suspected something seriously wrong.

Ew.

Still, both her parents were very attractive people. Positively dazzling, in fact, and thoroughly admired by their friends and coworkers alike. The dynamic duo was like neighborhood royalty. As was their due, Tracey supposed. After all, the Donners were a power couple.

They had worked hard to get where they were,

and they ruled the Gold Coast of Lower Fairfield County. Her mother sat on the board of several organizations supposedly dedicated to charity, but Tracey knew it was never about the actual charity.

The men and women involved in those things did it more to suck up to one another and to forge connections to further the careers of spouses and loved ones. Most of the very wealthy couples in that affluent neighborhood worked in or out of Manhattan, and sometimes Boston. Her father used to have offices in both cities, as well as connections in London, Paris, Berlin, and Rome. Alas, that was years ago.

When you were as rich as the Donners, you simply retired early and lived off your interests. Tracey often wondered why her parents didn't travel more, but she knew her mother would never leave Connecticut. Daniella Donner had worked too hard to be at the top of the in crowd. A crowd that had always made her daughter feel like an outcast.

The Gold Coast had its own brand of snobbery, and Tracey had never fit in with her mother's hoity toity friends. She preferred art and literature to wine tasting and jewels.

Tracey's idea of a good time involved sifting

through flea markets and exploring old churches. Things like that often horrified her staid parents.

"Tracey!" Her mother's shrill voice interrupted her train of thought, and she jumped, dropping the shoe box she'd been holding.

"I swear, child. You never have any idea what's going on."

"Sorry," she apologized, her eyes darting to the shoe salesperson who'd just returned with the next round of sandals—all of which were probably in the wrong size.

The fact they were not alone didn't seem to stop her mother. She hissed, narrowing her eyes like some feral cat, and Tracey braced herself for what was coming.

"Maybe if you paid a little more attention, you'd be able to lose some of that extra weight you gained this past winter. Maybe then Felix wouldn't have left you sitting in that restaurant to eat alone. How could you? I can't even imagine! Making a spectacle of yourself like that. You could have just left without eating, Tracey," she snapped the last bit with just enough venom that Tracey's stomach clenched.

"Left me? For your information, I asked him to leave, Mother. It was our first outing together, and since I had already ordered, he left, and I stayed.

What is so wrong with that?" Tracey asked, swallowing her gasp at the very real hurt that hit her harder than usual at her mother's cruel words.

Typically, she could ignore her mother's harsh commentary. But after her last relationship had ended in disaster, she was feeling vulnerable. And honestly, it was her mother's fault.

She'd started a relationship with Felix online without ever really seeing him. Those little avatars everyone used on social media were fun, but Tracey had never thought about it as hiding who she was until the man she thought she knew threw it in her face.

"You know, you have a pretty face. But you're a lot fatter than I expected. Since your mother and my mother are club friends, I thought you would be fit. But now I see why you have an avatar as your profile picture."

Felix's hurtful comment was like a slap in the face. Not only had she ended the date immediately after he'd said those hateful words, but she blocked his ass on every social media account.

Jerkface.

CHAPTER 2

Of course, Tracey could always count on her mother to pick at scabs. She heaved a sigh as her mother's pinched face grew even tighter.

"Well, you say tomato," her mother hissed, wincing as she used a shoehorn to squeeze into a tight pair of Manolo Blahnik mules.

"What does that even mean, Mother?"

"Dieting was never your strength, but you can turn that around with some work, Tracey. Then maybe you can catch a husband."

"Gosh, you make a man sound like a disease," Tracey whispered her reply.

"Your father is trying to persuade the governor to give the proposed expansion of the highway to his friend with that development company. What is his name? Oh, yes, Jeb Collins. He has a son named Trevor. If your father succeeds, there will be plenty of mingling with their family."

"So what, Mother?"

"So, he might make a match for you. And you can do your part by losing a few pounds. You know, bathing suit season is here—Gertie! You're here!"

Her mother greeted her rail thin best friend with air kisses and pats on the shoulder.

"Darling! Oh! Those are cute," Gertie said, eyeing a pair of silver wedges her mom had discarded.

She did not acknowledge Tracey, which was par for the course. Not that she minded. She disliked most of her mother's friends.

"Jeb Collins is eighty, and any son of his is probably fifty or older."

"He's fifty-three, Tracey, but what would you have me do? You'll be thirty soon—"

"Oh my god, Mom," she growled, frustrated. "I am thirty! I don't know that man. And what are you saying, you would what, sell me to him?"

"Hardly, dear," her mother replied, her pinched face looking even angrier than usual. "He would be doing *us* the favor, not the other way around."

Gertrude snorted into her elbow at the cruel jibe, and Tracey's humiliation doubled.

"That's not funny," Tracey responded with as much dignity as possible.

"It was not meant to be," her mother responded.

Tracey's whole body tensed with hurt and disgust for her parent.

"What happened to you, Mom? Why are you like this? You were never kind and loving like the other kids' parents when I was in school. In fact, I don't think you even like me."

"What are you talking about? Get a grip, Tracey."

"Get a grip? All you do is make snide comments about my appearance and rude remarks about me being single."

"Am I wrong? Look at you. You are at least forty pounds overweight. You don't care at all about our image. And as for the other, I am trying to help you."

"I happen to like how I look, Mom. And the last time I listened to you about a man, he cut me up with his cruel remarks about my weight. I don't need a man like that—"

"What are you talking about? Without a man, what will you be?"

"How about happy, Mom? I don't need a man to complete my identity," she said, ignoring her mother's cruel laughter.

Gertie said something waspish, and she and

Daniella cackled at whatever thinly veiled insult she'd just thrown at Tracey. But something was happening to her she'd never felt before. Her body was buzzing, her head pounding, and for the first time, she understood she would never be happy until she freed herself.

"Where are you going?" her mother asked as she gathered her purse and the bottle of water she'd been carrying.

"I'm leaving, Mom. You know, I happen to like myself just the way I am."

"Oh please," the older woman snorted.

"You know, I am very sorry for you that you never took the time to get to know me because now it's just too late. Goodbye, Mother."

"Tracey, you are being ridiculous. Get back here!"

But it really was too late. Tracey had already decided. She was closing the door on years of hurt and disappointment, gathering her last bits of hope and courage and holding them tight to her chest. Tracey turned one last time to take in her mother's posh appearance and cold expression.

"You're supposed to love and accept me no matter what. I am your daughter. That's what mothers do. How can you sit there and make fun of me?"

"Don't be so sensitive. Come now. We can find you a one piece to wear to the club. Maybe Jeb will be there. Here," she said and turned to find the saleswoman who'd been helping them since they entered the expensive department store.

"Janie, please find Tracey something suitable for this weekend's clam bake."

Clam bake was a bougie term for the extravagantly catered affair her mother was throwing to celebrate her father's one year retirement anniversary. They had an image to uphold, after all.

Tracey got nauseous just thinking about it. Her mother hadn't heard a single word she'd said.

"Of course, Mrs. Donner—"

"No need, Janie. I am not staying."

"Tracey, do not embarrass me in public—"

"You did that all by yourself, Mother. Goodbye Gertrude, Janie," she said, nodding at each red-faced woman. "Oh, and Mother, I won't be home for your clam bake this weekend. I have other plans. Tell my father congratulations for me."

Her heart thundered like a thousand runaway horses running down a hillside. The sound echoed in her ears. She couldn't believe she was doing this. But it was past time, she supposed.

Tracey pulled her cell phone out of the big boho

bag she'd fashioned herself out of 100% organic cotton fabric colored with vegetable dyes. The patchwork pattern formed an image of her favorite animal, a large wolf baying at a yellow moon with twinkling stars she'd made out of glass beads.

The result was a sturdy, fun, and bright bag that was perfect for summer. Tracey opened an app and ordered an Uber to meet her at the small café on the corner of the department store.

Unfortunately, in her thirty years on the planet, she'd never learned to drive. An oversight she was determined to correct that summer. Might as well, since she wouldn't be spending it at home. Closing her eyes, she dialed Rosa, the Donner's longtime housekeeper, next.

The woman had practically raised Tracey. If anyone was going to miss her, it would be the feisty little woman who had taught her sewing and embroidery. She also taught Tracey how to wash her clothes and how to cook at least a dozen different varieties of homemade empanadas.

Rosa was her rock. She was the one who comforted Tracey whenever life got hard, or her parents had upset her—which was often.

"Donner residence," she answered the phone.

"Rosa? It's me. I was just calling to let you know I won't be home for dinner."

"Okay, *linda*. Anything else?" Rosa asked, calling her the same endearment, meaning pretty, as she had ever since Tracey was a child.

Rosa was probably the only person who showed her any real affection. Ever cheerful and ready with a hug or compliment. God, she loved that woman. Tracey's heart pounded. She couldn't just leave without giving her an explanation.

"Actually Rosa, I won't be coming home till, *well*, I don't really know when. I'm, um, making a change," she said, her voice trembling.

"Are you okay? What happened, my Tracey?"

"I'm okay. I mean, I'm thirty years old. Mean words shouldn't have the power to hurt me anymore."

"Words do have power, *linda*. But I agree, it's time you take your power back."

Tracey sniffed and cleared her throat. Leave it to Rosa to give her strength when her own faltered. She smiled, her vision blurring with unshed tears.

"You're right. I'll be fine. Don't worry."

"Of course, I worry about you, silly. Who else would if not me? Now, tell me where you are going, so I don't worry too much."

"Um, I am going to the beach," she said on impulse.

"The beach? Well, good. But be careful. The beach is full of men looking to take advantage of a pretty and innocent girl like you. Wait a second, *mija*, don't listen to me. If a sexy man comes along, you have my permission to say yes," Rosa told her.

"Rosa!"

"What? Look, if someone does approach you, who knows? He could be just what you need. Like someone from those books you love to read."

"Rosa, have you been looking through my tablet again?" Tracey teased.

"You know I love those sexy stories. You could meet a mystery man, an oil sheik in disguise, looking for a princess to call his own, ooh yes! Or a pirate coming to whisk you away on his ship to ravage your body. *Si, linda*, you need some of that in your life."

"Oh my God! Rosa! You are banned. Stop reading all my smutty romance novels without supervision, young lady," Tracey mock scolded.

Her cheeks were burning from embarrassment, which was silly because no one could hear her conversation. Besides, at least she was laughing now.

"Smut is fun, Tracey. Besides, it happens. I was

just reading the one where the male escort decides he wants a woman to keep him in a fine condo and Armani suits, but then he falls in love with her and does his best to win her heart and trust after his lies come out. Anyway, never mind. Listen to me carrying on now," Rosa said and sighed wistfully.

"I'm going to miss you, Rosa."

"I will always be with you, *linda*. Whatever happens, you can do this. It is past time you ran away from this cold home, my Tracey."

"I know. You are right," Tracey answered, smiling through her tears. "I love you, Rosa."

She did, truly and deeply. Rosa Marquez was the only real mother she had ever known.

"I love you too, my Tracey. It will all be okay. Now, you text me on this fancy phone you got me for Christmas when you get to where you are going. You hear me? And if you decide not to come back, send me an address and I will make sure your things arrive safe and sound."

Relief and nervousness warred within Tracey as she nodded her head, ever the obedient child. She'd always been so eager to please Rosa, and why wouldn't she be? The woman had done nothing but reward her hard work with affection and honesty in ways her own parents had failed to do.

"Yes, Rosa. I will. Let me go before I change my mind."

"Don't do that now, *linda*. You are so close to finding yourself. May flights of angels protect and guide you, my Tracey."

"You too, Rosa. Bye."

Tracey clicked end call and walked to the corner as the Uber she'd ordered pulled into a vacant space. The man looked normal, and the car was spotless.

This was it. The moment of her great getaway.

"You Tracey Donner?" The older man asked.

"That's me."

"Where you headed?"

"Maccon City," she said, surprising herself with the certainty she heard in her voice.

"That's three hours away," the man said, eyebrows raised. "Your reservation said you were going ten minutes away—"

"I'll give you five hundred dollars cash," she said, cutting him off.

"Yeah? Well, okay then," he readily agreed.

Tracey nodded and stepped inside the car before she could chicken out. She had always been a home-body. Went to the nearest college and even finished her degree online. Her parents were not abusive.

Not exactly. They were a little cruel, but that was

because they just did not understand her. She could never live up to their impossible standards. It was time she admitted the truth, even if only to herself. Tracey was tired of trying.

Her childhood had been a series of disappointments for both her parents and for herself. When she was twelve, she had wanted to go to this sleep-away summer camp for art, instead they sent her to a weight loss camp for obese children.

Yes, Tracey had been pudgy even then. And when she'd returned from camp after spending a miserable six weeks there, she had actually gained three pounds.

Total. Failure.

It took her a long time to love herself after that. And the one thing she could always say whenever her mother harped on her weight was at least she was healthy, even if her mom thought she was unattractive. Tracey's yearly physicals and blood tests always came back with proof she was eating healthy, if a little more than her mother thought was okay, and she was exercising regularly.

She was just a big girl, for fuck's sake. The world was not going to end because Tracey Donner wasn't a size zero—*someone should tell that to her mother.*

But fat camp was not the end of her long list of

ways she'd disappointed her folks. When she'd graduated from high school, she'd refused to attend Boston College, or her mother's alma mater, Smith College, and opted for art school.

Her parents were so angry, they'd refused to pay. Luckily, a great-uncle on her father's side that she had never met had bequeathed her his entire estate when he had passed away years before. She was not rich, per se—especially not after paying her tuition. But Tracey had her own money, and it was past time she used it to live her own life.

"Time to find my place in the world," she whispered.

"What was that?" the driver asked.

"Nothing," she answered.

Biting her lip, she watched the scenery fade as she embarked on this, her first journey as an adult. Tracey had never been reckless or foolish. But there was a first time for everything. Maybe that was why she'd asked to go to the one place she remembered she was truly happy growing up.

Maccon City, New Jersey.

Rosa had taken her there for the weekend when she was thirteen and her parents had been away on vacation. How she'd loved that buzzing ocean side town!

Something was missing in Tracey Donner's life. She'd allowed her mother to bully and boss her around. She'd let her father's disapproval weigh her down. She had neglected her own wants and needs for way too long.

Time to start living for myself.

CHAPTER 3

Go. Go. GO!

Phoenix Tala jumped on his Screamin' Eagle V-Rod and hightailed it out of the *Serious Moonlight* parking lot. His inner Dire Wolf was chomping at the bit.

He'd always been able to sense and hear his animal inside his mind's eye. The relationship between every Shifter and his beast was different, but Phoenix would have it no other way. Two minds, one body—and no one knew him better than the enormous buff colored monster snarling and scratching inside of him.

His animal was desperate to get on the road. About a year had passed since the Dire Wolf MC—

that was what they called his Pack, so the normals around them did not grow suspicious—had settled down on the outskirts of Blue Valley, New Jersey.

It was the longest Phoenix had ever spent in one place. A full year of the same scenery and crowds. The same boring routine.

Okay, that was not exactly fair. He was proud of them and the success they had with their roadhouse and bar, *Serious Moonlight*. They'd opened their doors with plans to cater to both normals and the surprisingly large supernatural community on the East Coast, and they'd done it.

The place was great. So was the old homestead that came with the property. They'd managed to renovate the almost dilapidated building, turning it into a bonafide Pack house in the neighboring lot. And that was not all they did. They converted the old barn into a multi-vehicle garage.

The Pack could work on their bikes in a safe and convenient location. Cole was their expert mechanic, but the rest of them muddled along just fine. In fact, Phoenix had just replaced his scratched-up old seat with a cushioned Tallboy, extra wide and deep, with a high back for a passenger.

Not that he had anyone to ride double with him, but whatever. The second he saw the black leather seat, he knew it was for him. Tinkering with his bike and working on the computer setup for their business kept him busy for the first few months.

He'd watched as new customers became regulars and faces grew familiar. It was an odd experience for him, and at his age, that did not happen very often.

Dire Wolves aged more slowly than most Shifters, with almost twice the lifespan. He might look thirty, but he was twice that. But Phoenix had never felt his age more than these past months as he watched his Alpha, and two of his Pack mates, get mated.

Sure, he was happy for them. Life was good for the Dire Wolf MC. But something was missing from his life. He'd felt it keenly over the last few weeks.

It was the call to the road. That same feeling every member of the larger, and mainly nomadic, Dire Wolf Pack had felt and was best described as an irresistible urge—an almost magnetic pull to get on the road. Like destiny was breathing down his neck until he couldn't stand it another minute.

He'd tried to resist. Really, he did. But it was impossible. The Wolf was growling constantly. The urge to Change into his fur two times a day was taking its toll.

"Derrick, I gotta run, man. Please, I need some time on the road."

"How long?"

"I dunno. A few weeks at least."

That was the sum of his conversation with his Alpha the night before. Inside, he'd been begging the big man to understand. Hurt thrummed through their Pack bond, but bigger than that was compassion. Derrick was a good, strong Alpha.

He would never poison their bonds by ordering Phoenix to stay. The Alpha had narrowed his eyes at his Wolf, measuring the seriousness of Phoenix's request. Then, he'd stepped around the polished bar and grabbed him in a fierce, backbreaking hug, more befitting a Bear. But Dire Wolves weren't like any other canid species, supernatural or otherwise. They were the oldest, biggest, baddest, and most powerful canid Shifters in the entire world.

Their natural dominance was tempered by their desire for solitude. Derrick Rand was a good Alpha, and Phoenix would follow the man anywhere. But it was time he moved on. Well, for a little while, anyway. This was his Pack, his MC, and he would never leave for good.

Yeah, he'd come home alright. Could be a month,

could be a year, but he would return. All he knew was he had to settle the wildness he felt growing inside and he couldn't do that there.

"Do what you need to, brother. We'll be here for you. All you have to do is call."

Phoenix packed his saddlebags and left before the sun came up the next day, having kept his goodbyes brief. Lord knew he couldn't handle any tearful platitudes from their Alpha fem. Lucy was expecting a cub in a couple of months, and that meant the woman was even more emotional than normal.

"You go find whatever it is you're looking for, Phoenix Tala, then haul your furry butt back home before this baby is born!"

"I promise, Lucy, I'll call you whenever I land somewhere, okay?"

"You better."

Getting back on the open road was like seeing an old friend after a long absence. With his supernaturally enhanced lifespan, sometimes days bled into the other. But it really felt like a long time since he and the prehistoric beast he shared his soul with had gone exploring.

He revved his engine, loving the power between his thighs as he ate up the miles fast and furiously.

Phoenix missed this. But missing the open road wasn't the real reason he'd felt so uneasy lately.

There was something else out there calling to him. Something he was looking for. He just had to find it.

Not it. Her.

His Wolf growled the words inside his head, and Phoenix had to agree, the creature was right. That was the real missing link. Phoenix's Dire Wolf was on a mission to find his fated mate.

Fuck.

He wasn't a mystic like Thor, or a ladies' man like Weylin. He had good points, though. Phoenix had a healthy respect for the opposite sex and for the Fates who predetermined mated pairs—as was one of their purposes and their right.

A lot of folks were mistaken, and thought the Fates took away free will. But Phoenix had been around long enough to know that was not true. Sure, the Fates could bring folks together, but will and commitment, bone deep affection, compromise, and plain old fashioned hard work—well, those were the things what kept mates together.

He'd been watching Derrick and Lucy, Sheila and Leo, and Ariella and Brock for weeks—the six of them seemed happy as a couple of pigs in mud.

Each was just wild for the other. Who knew love could be so damn fun? But watching them, Phoenix learned it really could be. He was happy for Derrick, Sheila, Brock, and their respective mates. The Fates had done a really good job finding mates for three of his favorite people in the world.

He just hadn't realized the cause of his unrest until right then. It was time for Phoenix and the Fates to get together and get him settled.

Well, shit.

Now, what did he do? Put out an ad? Troll the bars? How the fuck was a rugged, rough-looking Dire Wolf like him gonna find a woman willing to settle down? Especially when he had nothing to offer a female.

What could he really give to a woman? Phoenix was not bad off, but he was not really wealthy either. The Pack had money, but he'd never put much stock in material things. He had a bedroom in the Pack house, his motorcycle, and a pretty sweet computer set up—but that was it.

Shit.

That was what happened when a man spent more time designing landscapes and avatar add-ons for online roleplaying games like *WolfMoon*—as was his side job for *Graves Enterprises*—than with building up his stock portfolio and buying property or what-ever the fuck people who wanted to have families did. What kind of woman would look at him and see a prize?

Fuck. Fuck. Fuck.

This was not like him. His Wolf snarled inside his chest, angry at him for selling them short. Maybe he was. After all, Phoenix wasn't a total loss. He was physically fit, had muscles chicks seemed to dig, and his face was okay, too.

His dick worked. That was a plus. And he knew his way around a female's body. Yeah, his communi-cation skills could use some work, but he was a guy. That was sort of their mo, right?

It wasn't that he was bad with women, he just never connected with them. He was not a stumbling virgin or anything. Dire Wolves, like most Shifters, were highly physical beings. Honestly, it had been a good, long while since he'd scratched that particular itch. But sex was like riding a bike. You didn't forget how to work the pedals just because it had been a while.

Now that he'd thought about it, he realized why the women who'd come on to him recently had been unappealing. His Wolf wanted his mate's touch. No other would do. But how should he approach this unique problem? He needed time and space to think this through. There was only one place that would offer the kind of atmosphere Phoenix needed to think. One environment that could help him plan and perhaps solve his little *mate-trimonial* dilemma.

Beach.

Grinning like the predator he was, Phoenix gunned his engine and sped towards the best damn shore town he'd ever visited in all his years.

Maccon City.

The Jersey shore town was home to the infamous Macconwood Pack—a cool bunch of Werewolves he'd had the pleasure of meeting a time or two.

Yesssss.

His Wolf sped him on, urging him to drive faster. Maccon City was perfect. He could just sit on the beach in the soft summer sand and contemplate his future, devise a plan to find and woo his mate. His chest vibrated with his beast's assenting growl.

Grrr.

For the first time in months, Phoenix felt energized and excited. Like he was headed for the ride of his life. He could almost taste the saltwater on the air despite the miles he had to go.

With a cocky grin and a rumble in his throat, he

sped down the hot asphalt with one thought in his brain—and it was set on repeat.

Mate.

Mate.

MATE.

CHAPTER 4

"What do you mean, you're full? You can't be," Tracey moaned.

She tried frowning hard at the young man behind the desk, but the guy looked like he honestly regretted telling her the news.

"I am very sorry, miss. But we are all booked."

Tracey closed her eyes and tried one of those deep breathing exercises she'd learned from the childhood psychologist her mother insisted she see.

Crap, she was bad at this. She exhaled quickly, almost passing out from lack of oxygen.

"Um, are you okay? What are you trying to do?"

"What? Yeah. Um, can you check again? I just need a minute," she mumbled, shaking her hands and pacing the small office.

"Of course," the young man replied with a sympathetic nod.

Crap. Oh damn. Ass. Shit. Fuck.

Ugh.

Tracey sucked at cursing, and at running away, too, apparently. What the heck was she doing here, anyway?

Doubts filled her mind as she stood in the small lobby of the Oasis Beachside Resort. It was newly renovated, charming really. She liked it better than all the glitzy hotels her family made them stay at when they'd gone away together, which was rarely.

Oasis was the last stop on the strip that ran along the beach, with private homes beside it, and a pathway to the pine barrens beside that. She hadn't been expecting this at all. In truth, she'd been pretty much unprepared for everything she'd encountered thus far.

It was already evening, and of course she couldn't find a room. It was August, for Pete's sake. Everyone was down the shore, trying to slow the last few days of summer. Tracey should have figured they would be crowded. Places like this depended on tourism to keep the economy going all year long.

Naturally, they were booked. Maccon City was a tourist favorite, especially with all the festivals, concerts, boardwalk craft fairs, and other events that took place every single weekend all summer long to keep the crowds happy. It made perfect sense.

She'd been one of them. A happy-go-lucky tourist from the second her Uber driver dropped her off. Unfortunately, she'd been so worked up over finally taking her independence back, she hadn't bothered to find a hotel. Not once on the whole drive down from Fairfield had she even considered looking for a place to stay.

Instead, she exited the car, wishing her driver safe travels back. Then she went shopping for some clothes and toiletries, even treated herself to an iced tea and fresh-baked lemon-blueberry scone.

Walking along the shop-lined streets was peaceful, relaxing even. She'd found the cutest little bead store and had talked with the owner for a full twenty-minutes about her purse and this idea she'd been toying with for her designs using glass beads and different texturized fabrics.

Sigh.

It had felt wonderful not to be looked down on for her craft. Her mother positively hated the fact that Tracey would rather make her own bag than buy an expensive designer one.

Double sigh.

Why hadn't she called for reservations first? Tracey was in such a rush to get away from her life, and her harpy of a mother, she hadn't been thinking clearly at all. Maccon City had always been a sanctuary in her mind, but the reality was she'd been neglectful.

Going home was the last thing she wanted, but what else could she do? Sleeping on the beach was illegal in New Jersey, not to mention totally unappealing.

"I am so sorry, miss. We are still booked. Have you tried the Seaside Escape?" the polite younger man asked.

"Yes, I went there first. This is the last place on the strip in the entire town, actually."

Could she really have messed this up so badly? This place was the last stop on the list of hotels she found on her phone for the whole of Maccon City.

She looked down at her smart phone's lit screen, but no matter how hard she stared, the words *no vacancy* refused to go away beneath every hotel name.

Crapola.

"Folks are here from all over the country this weekend, you know, for the festival. I'm Marco, by the way," he said.

Marco was nice enough, and a manager too, according to the little pin he wore on his shirt. He smiled and pointed to the framed poster displaying sailboats and smiling tourists under a banner with *Maccon City Annual Boat Show* splashed across the top.

Apparently, it was a big deal. The festival lasted the whole weekend and there was even a food truck festival, fireworks display, and a discount bracelet day on the pier for the rides to celebrate it.

Double crapola.

Tracey huffed a sigh and closed her eyes for a moment. She just couldn't believe it. Of all the stinking luck. The sound of the lobby door opening was distant, but she registered the fact that she was not alone with the friendly manager any longer.

She huffed a sigh and moved over to allow the newcomer access to the man. This was so like her. Tracey cringed at what her mother would say. Something about how irresponsible she was, for sure. And for the hell of it, the woman would throw in something having to do with her weight, because obviously that was why anything bad happened to her.

Stop it.

She shook her head, slightly admonishing herself

for the unkind thoughts. It was better to simply avoid thinking about her parents at all than to harp on the negative. It was not her mom's fault she hadn't even bothered to call for a reservation the whole drive from the North Shore. She was fine owning it, but it sucked.

Huffing out a frustrated sigh, she wondered what she should do next. Maybe just take in the scenery, then she could try the next shore town for a vacancy. It wasn't what she wanted, but it was a plan.

At least Marco, along with every other guy she'd spied during her search for a room, was good to look at. Maccon City was positively crawling with hotties.

The Oasis hotel manager was too young for her, but she could appreciate his beauty all the same. Someone cleared their throat, and she turned her head to the right just as she took a sip from her now warm bottle of water. That was a mistake.

Tracey damn near spit all over herself as she took in the enormous male standing there. If young Marco was cute, then the outrageously tall blond with piercing green eyes, and more muscles than she knew the human body could have, was positively stunning—in a totally drop dead gorgeous, way out of Tracey's league, kind of way.

"Hi," she said, once she'd swallowed, eyes wide.

The man frowned at her, like not a sad frown but a look of intense thought and concentration. It was actually kind of scary, so she turned to Marco.

"You don't mind if I sit here while I call some other hotels and look for a car?" she asked.

"Of course not," Marco replied easily, though his gaze was fixed on the stranger.

The strange yet beautiful man seemed to have a tickle or something in his throat. She sat down as far from him as she could get. He was making all kinds of weird grumbling noises, and she sincerely hoped he wasn't sick. That was the last thing she needed. To catch a virus or bug. But it would be just her luck.

Deciding to mind her own beeswax, Tracey started scrolling nearby towns. She wasn't having much luck, though. More grumbling, and some whispers sounded to her left, but she ignored the two attractive men.

Maybe Rosa was right. Maybe this place was full of hotties, looking for a rich chick to sidle up to.

Maybe I should take out an ad and try to find one. It would read, chubby heiress looking for fuckboy to give her multiple Os and cuddles. Will pay for rent and food.

Great, Tracey. Just great.

She was losing her freaking mind. There were no

male escorts searching for someone like her in Maccon City. And if there were any, surely, they were busy. Besides, she wasn't the type of woman who could pay for pleasure.

Then again, desperate times.

She laughed out loud, ignoring the stares of the two men in the lobby. Hell, she was entitled to her little freak out. Everyone thought she was nutty, why not them?

No explanations were forthcoming or necessary.

Tracey was in semi-panic mode. True, this train of thought was not helping, but she was on a roll now. Was it too late to turn back?

Yes. Probably. Definitely. Dang it.

Was she sweating? Why was it so hot? She sucked in a breath and exhaled slowly to try to calm her growing hysteria. Was the air condition not working?

One flick of her gaze to the vent in the ceiling told her air was coming through, but boy, was she hot! Her skin was on fire. Maybe that growly hot guy really was sick. Maybe he gave her some kind of cold or flu!

Yeah, Tracey, and you got sick ten seconds after meeting him. What is wrong with you?

She breathed again, aware of eyes on her. But

Tracey was used to being regarded as a freak. She stared down at her phone. Maybe she could find a room to rent in someone's house if she couldn't find a vacancy at a hotel.

That was a new idea, and a much better one than paying for a night of companionship. Her cheeks were burning, but she played it off like she wasn't having some sort of psychotic break in the tiny lobby of the Oasis hotel. She searched frantically for rental properties, hardly aware she was being addressed.

"Um, miss. Miss?"

"What? Oh! Sorry," she mumbled, dropping her phone in her haste to face Marco.

"Sorry, miss—"

"Tracey. My name is Tracey," she replied, bending down to grab her phone. "Hey, do you know if anyone has a room to rent? I'm sorry for just sitting here, and taking up your space—"

"Please, make yourself comfortable, Tracey," a deep, unfamiliar voice said.

Wowza.

She almost dropped her cell phone again at the sound of her name spoken in an impossibly sexy voice. Ripples of shocking awareness spiked through her as Tracey looked up into a pair of sparkling green eyes.

Like Columbian emeralds, she thought. More aqua than green. So much more intricate than any other pair of eyes she had ever seen. Complicated, in fact.

The color was so unique it was almost indescribable. The artist in her was floored by the way they seemed to change before her own eyes. Aquamarine, then gold, then bright bottle green, and back to sea foam green.

Beautiful.

"I studied a book on eye color once, when I was researching my own boring muddy jade color, my parents are both blue-eyed. Anyway, the book had thousands of pictures of different colored eyes, but I don't recall coming across anything like yours."

"Pardon?" the stranger said, cocking his head to the side.

"Your eyes. They're, *um*, unusual. Pretty," she said, clearing her throat.

"Thank you, Tracey. No one's ever called me pretty before," the handsome man replied.

He looked amused, not angry, with his eyes tracing her face and his head still tilted to the side. He reminded her of a stray dog she fed by the house when she was younger.

"I guess not. Sorry," she murmured.

The poor animal kept coming back, and he would wait, head cocked to the side just like this, to see if Tracey would hurt him or not. Of course, she never did. Just gave him bits of her food. Her mother had found out and called animal control to take him away.

"Don't apologize. I like it," he said, but she was too stuck in her head to answer right away.

That was not a happy memory. She'd been trying to figure out why she'd not been blessed like her parents with crystal blue eyes, but she pushed away any sadness the memory evoked as she tried to find her voice to answer the strangely beautiful man.

It was like a whole universe existed in his gaze. The green was positively glowing with inky swirls of blue swimming in the depths. His face was tense, but she could sense his patience and innate goodness.

"You do?"

"I do."

"Oh," she said, dumbly.

It must be his aura, getting her all mixed up. He was a dominant personality, and she was a mouse. But despite his innate power, he was being patient and gentle. Kind, even. She didn't know what to make of him.

"I think you're pretty too, Tracey," he said.

"Oh, you don't have to—I mean, thank you," she mumbled, telling herself it was alright to accept a compliment.

"Just lovely," he said.

His voice was even better than his face, which was almost too good to be true. He had a face artists would kill to sketch. Tracey was more of a craft person, but even her fingers were itching for a pencil.

"Thanks," she whispered.

The sound was more sigh than statement. Not at all like her. Tracey didn't fawn over men, no matter how sexy they were.

"I believe Marco has found you a vacancy in the hotel."

"Oh? Really! You did?" She shook her head, breaking eye contact and turned to Marco, who was watching the byplay with more than a little interest.

"Uh, yeah. Last minute cancellation," the younger man said and nodded.

"Perfect!"

The stranger left the lobby and though she didn't want him to go, she hardly had cause to ask him to stay. With any luck, she'd see him around the place.

"Credit card?" she asked and handed Marco her Visa.

"Thank you. Let's get you entered here," he said.

Tracey felt both elated and anxious. She had no idea why, but she felt as if everything was finally working out. It was like Maccon City had called to her, and yeah, it was bumpy at first, but she'd come to the right place.

"Can I get you anything else?"

"No, I think I'm going to be just fine," Tracey told the hotel manager, accepting her key with a wide grin.

And for the first time in her life, she meant it.

You're free to be happy, Tracey.

CHAPTER 5

"She's here," Phoenix growled into his cell phone.

"Who?" Thor, his Pack mate, asked.

"It's her, bro."

"Phoenix, I have no idea what the fuck you are talking about," growled the baldheaded Wolf in reply.

Fuck. He was right. Phoenix should probably start at the beginning.

"Where are you, bro? You left with like no fucking warning."

"I'm at the *Oasis* in Maccon City."

"By the Macconwood Pack?"

"Yeah man, look, I fucking found my mate. She's human."

"Human?" Thor asked, and Phoenix's Wolf growled in response to the perceived judgement.

His animal side did not always have patience for his Pack mates, even if the man knew better. Thor was not being judgmental. Other Shifter species chose humans as their mates all the time. But that was not the case with Dire Wolves.

"Yeah, human and fucking perfect," he grunted.

"Alright, man. So, have you talked to her?"

Such a simple question and so loaded. Phoenix had a hard time controlling his instincts when he first spied her talking to the young Macconwood Wolf, who happened to be the manager at the hotel.

"Not really," he grumbled.

"Why the fuck not?"

"Because. I don't know!"

Phoenix muffled another curse as Thor remained silent on the line. He could count on the Pack Enforcer to have his back, but Thor was more than that. The Wolf was touched by the Gods, gifted—a Seer. Rare even among their kind, he needed the man's insight to let him know if he was on the right track.

"I need a minute," Phoenix growled, his Wolf pushing hard.

As he expected, Thor remained silent. He was good Pack, a good man—the very best.

Phoenix wrestled with his Wolf. He replayed recent events in his head. The sudden road trip and the unease his Dire Wolf had been feeling just lately —all of it had led him here, to Maccon City.

He'd stayed at the Oasis before, knew it was run by the Beta of the Island Stripe Pride and his Wolf Shifter mate. They served many supernaturals there, able to provide safety and secrecy their kind needed.

"Bro, I hate to cut this short, but I gotta go on an errand for Derrick. Say what you need to say."

Thor's voice brought him back to the present, and Phoenix closed his eyes and tried to focus his scattered mind. He saw her in his mind's eye. His beautiful mate. He really had found her.

She was so damn beautiful. His Tracey—such a simple name for such a complex person. He could sense she had more layers to her than met the eye, and he couldn't wait to reveal them all.

Mine.

"I met a woman here. My fated mate, Thor. She is the one," he told the other man confidently.

Once he said it aloud, he felt as if the entire world shifted two degrees. He felt lightheaded, dizzy, but once it settled, Phoenix knew this was right.

The tiny human female was his destiny. His Dire Wolf tossed his head back and howled into the metaphysical plane where he dwelled, alerting the entire MC through their pack bonds that he'd found his one and only.

"Wow. I felt that shit, bro. I am really happy for you. Did she accept you right away?"

"That was the reason I called. I haven't told her—"

"Fuck. Phoenix, bro. That part is complicated, but it is vital to your journey."

"I know. Got any advice?"

"I don't know from personal experience, but from what I've seen, you just gotta be honest. Don't be quiet about your feelings, yeah? Stay safe, bro."

"Thanks, man. You, too."

Be honest.

Seemed simple enough. And yet, not so simple. Phoenix was positive Tracey was human. She wouldn't know anything about Shifters and fated mates. How the hell was he going to break it to her?

It wasn't like he could just walk up to her and reveal the truth about the supernatural world and have her jump into his sometimes furry arms. Fuck.

How was he ever going to convince her to give him a chance?

Phoenix ended the call and went back to his room. He needed to devise a plan, like now. From the displeasure he'd seen on that pup manager's face when he'd all but insisted the female be given a room on the unofficial Shifter only rooftop of the resort, Phoenix figured he had less than a day to get the curvy goddess up to speed.

The young Wolf, Marco, had only given in after Phoenix had allowed his own beast to shine through his gaze. His Dire Wolf was more dominant than the younger male, but Phoenix knew without being told he was going to be dealing with someone from the Macconwood Pack Wolf Guard, or maybe even the Alpha himself, eventually.

Shit.

Derrick was going to be pissed. Phoenix would just have to explain what the situation was when they came knocking on his door, as they undoubtedly would.

He ran a hand through his hair and tried to regain his composure. It wasn't like he could just rush out there and jump on the woman. No matter what his Wolf thought.

Sniff, bite, hello mate.

Yeah. Right. Not happening.

He rolled his eyes at his silly animal's ideas on wooing the female. Listening for any sign of her, he decided it was stupid to stay in his room. But he couldn't pretend to sit by the pool in his present getup. Phoenix tore off his jeans and boots, opting for a bathing suit, tank top, and a pair of Crocs bearing the *Serious Moonlight* logo before heading out to the rooftop infinity pool.

Say whatever you want about the rubber footwear, they were the most comfortable things he'd ever felt on his size fourteens. And yes, he'd groveled apologetically at Sheila's feet after the woman had gifted each of their Pack a pair of the things, along with the tank top he had on and other swag items bearing the roadhouse's name.

"Oh, wow. This is gorgeous!" Tracey's voice floated over to him, and he turned, eyes landing on her immediately.

She was standing in the doorway of her room, right next to his, and *oohing* and *aahing* over everything appreciatively. Odd, she had no luggage, only one large, rather pretty bag on her shoulder.

Marco was saying something to her that caused her to smile amid the rambunctious pups and cubs running and jumping into the pool. He supposed it was going to be difficult to hide what they were from her. But with any luck, he wouldn't have to for long.

Thor's words replayed in his head, and Phoenix trembled with anticipation—or was that fear? Fuck, if he knew.

Be honest.

His stomach clenched, muscles bunched and at the ready. He frowned, realizing his Wolf did not like how close Marco, the young and handsome hotel manager, stood next to her. In fact, he was considering rearranging the smaller man's face before he caught himself stepping towards the pair of them,

Shit. He needed to get a grip on himself. The young Wolf was only showing her how to use the key card. Once she was inside, Marco turned and walked back to Phoenix.

Here it comes, he thought with a grin.

"I've placed Miss Donner in the room next to yours, as you requested. I'm sure you are aware we don't usually allow normals up here, Mr. Tala."

"I am aware. Thank you for accommodating my request."

"Protocol dictates I inform my Pack."

"I understand, and have you?"

"Yes."

"Very good. When you talk to them again, as I know you will, make sure you tell them the human woman is my fated mate, and I have every intention of informing her by the end of the weekend."

Marco held his gaze a beat longer than he expected, and Phoenix grinned at the younger man's tenacity. Good for him.

"That would probably be wise. Good luck, Mr. Tala."

"Thanks. I might need it," Phoenix replied, jaw dropping when his soon-to-be woman came back outside with her hair hanging down her back in soft waves.

She was wearing a black bathing suit and a sheer sarong that molded to her ample curves and made his inner beast stand up and take notice.

Holy fuck.

The woman was a knockout. His heart pounded in his chest, the sound of his blood pumping through his veins was louder than the crash of waves against the sandy shore.

Thump thump. Thump thump. THUMP THUMP.

CHAPTER 6

Phoenix growled deep in his throat. Tracey slipped past him, and a burst of her natural fragrance invaded his nostrils. Her scent was heavenly. Like freshly laundered cotton and blossoming fields of daisies.

Natural. Unique. Untainted.

He sucked in air greedily, but she was already gone. Whatever of her scent that lingered nearby, it wasn't enough. The beast went into hunter mode, and Phoenix took the stairs two at a time. Where had she gone? How long had he stood there, immobile, and frozen in place?

Fuck.

Summer afternoons were notoriously long on

the East Coast. The sun was still shining brightly in the sky, but the beach was nearly empty. Afternoon crowds were headed to the pier for more of the local festivities, carnival rides, and boardwalk snacks.

Phoenix scanned the horizon. Cars drove past, playing loud music with eardrum breaking bass making his Wolf snarl. Families and couples milled about, searching for food and fun. A flock of seagulls called and dipped down from the air, plucking French fries from a forgotten container tossed carelessly on top of a trash can.

He jogged across the street from the hotel to the beach, snarling at a car that took the corner too fast and screeched to a halt in front of him. The older driver honked the horn and looked ready to curse, but seemed to change his mind when he met Phoenix's angry glare.

Grrrr.

Typically, he did a better job at hiding his Wolf. But the animal was right pissed with him. Angry at his human side for losing their mate.

It wasn't a good idea for him to be outside when he was less than a hundred percent in control. But he couldn't run back to his hotel room now. Not until he found her.

Warm sand greeted his bare feet as he reached the shore, and Phoenix squinted against the glaring rays of the sun. This semi-private strip of beach belonged to the hotel and was marked off by ropes and a stand for lounge chair and umbrella rentals. There was also a row of a dozen potted palm trees and a small tiki hut selling fresh fruit and drinks.

The area had cleared out since this morning. All the families with young children and couples looking for entertainment had already left to prepare for the evening's delights. Boardwalk fries with malt vinegar, carousel rides, and carnival games, he could only imagine. Would Tracey enjoy a visit to the boardwalk? Would she enjoy rides or sharing cotton candy? He couldn't wait to find out.

Suddenly, he stilled. Phoenix closed his eyes, allowing his preternatural senses to push forward as he filtered through the lingering smells of suntan oil, picnic lunches, salty air, and beach traffic. There. He opened his eyes, head whipping around to find his tantalizing Tracey standing near the surf.

There she is.

His Wolf growled softly, the beast pressed him to move. But Phoenix stood his ground, just watching her. Relief filled him at the mere sight of the delicious woman.

She was completely safe and sound, walking with her sandals held high and a smile on her pretty face as the waves tickled her feet with their foam and teasing little laps. He admired her from afar. Just breathing in the same air she did seemed to settle his beast.

Damn, she was beautiful. She had a steady confidence that called to him. Like she was utterly and completely happy in her own skin, and fuck, wasn't that attractive?

Phoenix drank in the sight of her greedily. She had curves for miles, and a smile that lit up the world. Outlined in the orange gold glow of the afternoon sun, Tracey Donner was a vision.

Everything else seemed to fade away as he stared. The entire world could have been swallowed up by a black hole, and Phoenix would have been totally unaware of it.

There was no noise. No seagulls or tourists. Even the ocean fell silent. All he could see, hear, breathe, was her.

Just her.

Mine.

She sat on the sand for a long while, just looking out at the sea. He felt like a voyeur, but fuck, if he could have moved, he would have. Phoenix was glued to the spot. Caught between wanting more and simply wanting to observe. Every nuance of expression, every sigh and gasp at the beauty surrounding her, were all stored away in the deepest recess of his mind.

She giggled when the water touched her bare toes. Scowled when a seagull dove too close to her face. Sighed when an elderly couple walked by holding hands like teenage lovebirds. Tracey was a romantic.

Good to know.

Time passed quickly, and the sun had already started to dip in the sky. Maybe he was a coward for not approaching her, but Phoenix did not regret the hours he spent taking her in at a distance. She stood up, dusting sand from her bottom, and walked farther down.

He followed her stealthily as she trekked along the surf to an even more deserted part of the Oasis' private beach. Bordering a sectioned off plot of sand that was sheltered from the public eye by high dunes and a sign that read *private property*, Tracey paused.

Phoenix wondered who owned the stretch of beach that forbade his mate entry, but he took a deep breath and got his answers. The private section carried the same Tiger and Wolf scents as the hotel.

It must belong to the owners of the Oasis, just like the mansion a few dozen yards away.

He crouched behind another row of potted palm trees, watching as Tracey glanced behind her before crossing into the private section of beach. He grinned in surprise. The little female was a rule breaker. He hadn't expected that.

Rebel rebel.

He knew the family was not home. His Wolf could sense it. Tracey was safe for now. He was curious to see how far she would go. So, Phoenix waited with bated breath, crawling on his belly past the dunes so he could get to her if she need help. He stayed out of sight, hiding his large frame behind some tall beach grass, just to see what she would do.

Holy fuck.

Phoenix never expected the cute as fuck little human to strip to her skin in public. He almost swallowed his tongue as she pushed her bathing suit down her body, revealing acres of creamy skin and ample curves.

Did he call her cute? Fuck that. She was gorgeous. Long, blonde hair fell down her back in waves reflecting sunlight like spun silver and gold thread, a myriad of colors, all of them breathtaking and precious. He was dying to run his fingers through those seductive, long locks.

Her hair hung past her shoulders, all the way down, teasing the dimples over her round, peach of an ass. Phoenix drooled. Like he actually fucking drooled.

Gulp.

CHAPTER 7

Wiping his mouth on the back of his hand, he tried to swallow his growl, but there was no containing his beast. He wanted her more than he wanted anything else in his entire life.

The briny ocean breeze was no competition for the fresh, warm scent that floated off her skin to his eager and sensitive nostrils. Like sugar cookies and warm vanilla. Sweet, delicious, and oh, so tempting.

Fuck.

He was going to lose the tremulous hold he had on his restraint. Already, his cock was stone hard, damn near punching a hole through his swim shorts. He hissed a breath as he adjusted himself. Somehow, afternoon had faded to evening, and the ocean glittered before them, inviting, but deadly. Everyone knew not to swim at this hour.

At least, he thought they did. Before he could yell a warning, Tracey dove into the waves, and he couldn't help himself. He had to join her. To protect her, sure, but also to be near her.

Phoenix took off his shirt and kicked off his sandals before diving into the water a good hundred feet away and out of her line of vision. The Jersey shore beach was calmer in August, and he was dazzled by the play of water clinging to her ripe breasts as she turned and floated on top of the waves.

She looked like a sea nymph or goddess, just gliding on the water with a soft, serene smile spread across her beautiful face. All he wanted to do was kiss her. His Dire Wolf urged him to go on. Hurry and claim her before someone else did, but he reined in his beast.

Hell. He couldn't just jump on the woman. In fact, he was pretty sure that was illegal. Plus, he did not want to frighten or overwhelm her. The sun dipped down lower, and the cool Atlantic grew dark. His senses were on alert, aware of the dangers that lurked.

Once more, he was reminded of the fact they

shouldn't be in the sea at this time of night. It was feeding time for beasts and other things. Subtle movement beneath the waves alerted him to the presence of a natural predator.

Fuck.

Tracey floated on, blissfully unaware of the danger, but Phoenix was already on the move. He pushed his body through the water, growling menacingly at the shark. The apex predator made no noise, but from his position beneath the darkening tide, Tracey must have resembled something tasty.

Too bad for the shark, the little vixen was spoken for. Phoenix lunged, bopping the bull shark on the nose, and the animal, sensing a hunter more vicious than he, swam away without further incident.

Watching to make certain the shark was not coming back, Phoenix forgot to pay attention to where he was. Tracey, the seductive siren, was still floating on her back, unaware of him—that was, until she swam right into his body.

Ooops.

Electrical charges charged through his blood at the inadvertent contact and whatever attraction he'd felt since first laying eyes on her amplified innumerably. Her strangled scream and consequential splashing had him swallowing a mouthful of salt water before he knew what happened.

"What the hell? Oh damn! I'm sorry, I thought I was alone!" Tracey gasped as he coughed and spit water.

"S'fine," he growled, hoping it played off as a result of swallowing saltwater. "You are alone. Just me, and a hungry shark."

"Shark?" She screeched again, making him hunch at the sheer decibel of her voice.

Tracey splashed backwards, looking around, and he immediately felt guilty for scaring her.

"No worries. He's gone now. I didn't mean to scare you," he said, trying his best not to stare at her pretty tip-tilted breasts.

"Well, you say shark, of course I'm gonna be scared. Say, is this some line you use to trick swimmers into being grateful to you? Hello? My eyes are up here," she snapped.

To his utter sadness, Tracey covered her luscious pink nipples with one arm as she moved into more shallow waters, and Phoenix had to bite back his growl.

What was wrong with him? He was acting like a dog with a new bone. She deserved better from him than to ogle her lady bits without permission.

He was downright fucking ashamed of himself and couldn't even help the growl that rumbled through him. Her shocked eyes met his, and he turned it into a cough. This was not like him. Phoenix had better control of himself than that.

Sorta. Maybe.

"Uh, what?" he asked.

"Never mind. I have an overactive imagination."

"Ookay," he mumbled, following her, but not too close.

He was stunned. Phoenix did not know what to say, and that was a fucking first for him. Her reactions had him completely flummoxed. Most women would scream and holler if a man found them naked in the ocean, but she didn't. In fact, she hardly seemed aware of her nudity.

"I suppose that's what I get for trespassing and thinking I was alone. Is this your place?"

"No," he replied, shadowing her as she moved towards the shore.

"Then you're trespassing, too."

"Yeah, I guess I am."

Awareness suddenly flashed between them, and Phoenix could sense her growing embarrassment. But it was slightly less than the curiosity he saw sparkling in her eyes. The two emotions seemed to war inside her, and he hoped like fuck the latter won out.

In fact, greedy bastard that he was, Phoenix was positively rooting for it. Tracey tilted her head, eyeing him once, then flitting her gaze to her clothes still sitting in a pile on the shore.

"I suppose I should thank you for saving me from the shark," she teased, and he knew she didn't believe him.

That was fine. It wasn't exactly important to the rest of their story, far as he was concerned. She did not have to know the truth about her near miss. She had the fealty of a monster now. His Wolf was already bonding to her, and they'd barely spoken two sentences to one another.

Amazing.

"My pleasure," he answered, and meant it.

"So, are you a gentleman or not?"

"Depends on what you mean," he answered.

"Well, we're both in here and I am assuming we are both naked—"

"I have on trunks," he replied, grinning at the pink blush that crossed her cheeks.

"Oh, well, that's not fair."

"Here, I'll even things up," he said, pulling them off and tossing them onto the shore faster than any human should be able to move.

Ooops.

"Wow. That was crazy," she murmured, eyes wide. "Okay, well, now that we are both naked, I propose I exit the water first and you, *kind sir*, avert your eyes."

"Are you kidding? Why would I do that?" Phoenix asked, perplexed.

"Because I don't even know your name. I'm not about to jog out of here and flaunt my fun bags and all my jiggly bits in front of you," she said with a giggle.

"In that case, my name is Phoenix Tala, and you are Tracey, I believe? I'm staying at the Oasis. I think I saw you there today," he replied with a grin.

"Yep, Tracey Donner," she said, and laughed. "And true, we might be introduced now, but turn around anyway, Phoenix Tala."

"Yes, ma'am. My mama raised me to be a gentleman, so I'll give you ten seconds before I even attempt to sneak a peek," he told her, only half-kidding.

"Oh, a mama's boy? I like that."

"Ha! I'll tell her you said that," he murmured.

"That's weird. We're strangers."

"Not anymore. You know my name now."

"True, Phoenix," she replied, biting her lower lip. "Okay, turn around. No peeking."

"I'll turn around, but no promises," he replied honestly.

He was an honest Wolf and wouldn't steal a look. Probably. Maybe. Hell, he sure wanted to.

"You are such a tease. Okay, here I go," she called, already swimming to the shore.

Phoenix bit the inside of his cheek and counted to twenty before turning around. He caught the sweet curve of her ass disappearing into her swimsuit and the sight was temptation itself.

"My turn to get out, I guess," he said, catching her wide-eyed stare.

"I won't look," she told him.

"I don't mind if you do.

He lingered, paddling slowly through the cool water. The moment was intense, and his Dire Wolf stirred inside of him. The very air seemed charged with feeling. She had all his attention, man and beast watched her with covetous eyes.

She pulled her straps over her arms, turning to face him boldly, and Phoenix's smile grew even wider. She was a knockout, and not just because of her looks. Tracey was brave and confident, and that was even better than all the glitter in the world.

"Here I come, little one," he growled, giving her one last chance to keep her modesty. But she didn't avert her eyes. In fact, she lowered them, staring at that part of him that so obviously wanted her.

"Wow," she whispered, but his Wolf ears picked up the word just fine.

A small gasp escaped her lips and Phoenix had never been so glad of his physical appearance as he was at that moment. He moved languidly, standing tall and proud as rivulets of water snaked down his skin. He allowed her to look her fill before he picked up his shorts and tank from the sandy shore.

"Oh my God, I'm a peeping Tom!" Tracey squeaked, turning her head.

"Don't you mean Tomasina?"

"I don't know. I suppose," she mumbled, and her embarrassment made her even more adorable.

Phoenix chuckled as he slipped his tank top over his head and grabbed his Crocs from the sand. Her blush deepened from pink to red, and he'd never seen anything so damn cute.

· · ·

"**I** should go," Tracey said, but she remained glued to the spot, as if she did not want to leave him just yet.

Good. That was good.

Phoenix did not want to go either. She was so sweet. Pretty and kind. Honest and brave. He wanted to know all her secrets. To learn everything he could about her. His Wolf growled and scratched, the animal wanted her too.

Fuck. No.

He didn't want her to leave. He wanted more time with her. He wanted everything. And he wanted it now. Patience never was his strong suit, but he needed to find some. She was a normal and would not understand his instinctual need for her. His certainty that she was it for him would likely look like some lame pickup line, and Phoenix did not want that at all.

"You wanna leave me, already? After all we've been through?"

"What?" she asked, a grin teasing the side of her mouth.

"I mean, I rescued you from a near shark attack and we went skinny dipping together. We're practically engaged."

"Oh my God! You did not just say that."

"It's true. What kind of woman plays with a man's emotions and then leaves him flat?

"Are you serious?"

"As a heart attack, Tracey Donner."

"Well, what can I do to repair your tainted view of me?" she teased.

"Well, I think you can start by letting me feed you."

"Feed me?"

"Yeah, Tracey. I wanna feed you. Come to dinner with me," he growled, eyes eating her up as she danced around, giving him an answer.

She was delightfully flustered, and he could tell she was wavering. Beautiful, smart, pretty little siren. He watched her come to a decision, marveling at her absolute cuteness, then braced himself.

"Okay, Phoenix Tala," she said, using his full name, and fuck, it sounded good falling from her lips.

Gonna sound even better when she screams it.

"Okay what? Is that okay yes or okay no?" he asked, anticipation making his chest pound even harder.

"Okay, I'll have dinner with you." Tracey said, gifting him with a megawatt smile just at the end.

And just like that, the female owned him. His

Dire Wolf scratched at his skin, the beast wanting her more and more. There was something different about her, and not just because she was his mate. She had this inner glow, like magic. It was like her soul was all lit up from within and his Wolf could see it.

He wanted it for himself—*selfish creature*. But he more than wanted her, he needed her. Phoenix already coveted the lovely female. His beast did, too. He wanted to protect her, to possess her, to get her so used to him she couldn't possibly leave.

Fuck, he was losing it.

Grrrrr.

CHAPTER 8

When Tracey left her new hotel room, the manager of the Oasis had suddenly found for her, her first thought was to go straight to the beach. So she did.

There was no one to tell her not to, after all. No one to remind her she was not beach body ready or to scold her choice of bathing suit. Years of Mother's constant criticisms were ingrained in her brain, but Tracey had been working hard to push them right out of her head.

She was her own person, and that might not be what Daniella Donner wanted in her daughter, but that was too bad for her uptight mother. Tracey was worthy of love and respect, and she deserved to be happy.

It was a hard lesson, learning happiness did not grow on trees. There would be no happy ever after within easy pickings for Tracey. But those were lessons she'd learned early. Tracey always knew she would have to endeavor to find her own happiness. Good thing she didn't mind a little hard work.

Giggling like a child as the cool Atlantic bathed her unpolished toes, she tried not to picture her mother. The woman who birthed her would be horrified her only child had failed to get a pedicure before stepping onto the beach. But Tracey didn't care.

In fact, she realized in the short time she'd been in Maccon City, a lot of her stress and anxiety were caused by the same thing. Fear of displeasing her parents. Blame them as she might want to, truth was, this was Tracey's fault. Her mother and father were not bad people, but she had failed to define her boundaries.

By not speaking up, she had allowed them to pick at her very soul. But no more. She needed time away from them so she could like herself again and get her feet on solid ground. It was a blessing that Tracey was financially independent.

Fact was, she did not require her parents'

approval to be happy. She could live her life as she saw fit, pursue her craft, and just be happy. Tracey was just not anything like her parents, and that was okay.

She was fine with being different. It didn't make her bad or less than in any way at all. She'd made peace with that a long time ago, and yet she'd failed to convey her feelings to the two people who should have cared about her most of all. Maybe her unfortunate confrontation with her mother had been necessary.

It was just the push she needed to go out there and do the things she liked and wanted to do with her life. It was scary leaving home, but she was a big girl in more ways than one.

"You're gonna be alright, Tracey," she told herself in a low whisper.

Maccon City had one of the prettiest beaches she had ever seen, and it was no wonder so many tourists flocked to New Jersey to visit every year. Tracey sat and watched the waves for hours, spying a pod of bottlenose dolphins a few hundred feet out into the blue Atlantic. The constant breeze was soothing to her soul, as were the warm rays of the afternoon sun. Children laughed, lovers held hands, and the ambience was like a balm to her hurts. She had definitely come to the right place.

Beautiful. Peaceful. Magical.

After a while, she stood and walked along the shore until she saw a private property sign. Feeling a little reckless, she continued on, making sure no one was around. Something about the water was just so inviting, enticing even.

In a completely uncharacteristic move, Tracey stripped off her cover up and bathing suit, allowing the summer wind to caress her warm, naked flesh.

The act was like making a statement. A proclamation that Tracey was in the here and now. She was alive and in the world. She was her own person. Worthy of love and respect. A familiar refrain played itself over and over in her mind.

I am woman. Hear me roar.

Tracey grinned and took off at a run, diving between the beckoning waves of the still cool Atlantic. Smiling and bursting with pride at her sheer nerve, Tracey kicked her feet and used her arms and hands to slice through the water in a clumsy breaststroke. She flipped over, floating on her back and allowed the water to surround her. She couldn't hear anything but the sound of her own breathing and the rapid beat of her heart with her ears beneath the surface, and that was fine with her.

The Atlantic was doing a good job, lifting her up and washing away all her cares and worries. It felt so good, so invigorating. The salt water caressed her naked skin, and wow, she felt so free without a stitch of clothing on.

How many times had she been taught to hide her body as if it were something shameful? How many times had her parents set her up with gym memberships, personal trainers, dieticians, and fat camps?

Some of her worst memories centered on her parents' reactions to her weight and body shape. She'd tried it their way for years, and even when she had lost weight, she never kept it off. Her body just seemed to like chub. What could she say?

She ate healthy almost all the time. Choosing fish over steak, plenty of leafy greens, lean poultry, whole grain breads, and the like—but yes, she also occasionally indulged in mint chocolate chip ice cream, chocolate covered strawberries, and coffee with cream.

She exercised, sorta. Tracey loved to go for walks and got a few miles every day, either outside or on the treadmill. She was a real woman with real curves. Tracey had friends who were thin and naturally slender, and they were still not a hundred percent happy with their bodies. The way she saw it, every body was a work in progress. And regardless of what Mother said, every body was a beach body, too. Yes, she carried some extra pounds, but she refused to feel sad about it.

Lost in her thoughts, Tracey did not realize she wasn't alone until she collided with what felt like a wall floating in the ocean—*albeit a warm, muscular, living wall.*

"What the hell? Oh damn! I'm sorry, I thought I was alone," she shrieked.

Tracey was completely mortified. How had she not seen this gorgeous man getting into the water?

Crap.

This was a private beach. Was it his? She had never done anything as reckless as this, but Tracey couldn't seem to help herself. With the sun dipping low in the sky as afternoon mingled with evening, she'd been sort of inspired—*and then she'd been caught.*

Double crap.

Tracey should get out. She couldn't, though. Holy hell, she had almost forgotten she was totally and completely naked. All her girly bits were hanging out. Thank goodness the water was not crystal clear. New Jersey had clean beaches, but the algae and whatnot tended to be more opaque than the tropics.

I AM NAKED WITH A STRANGER. OMG. OMG. OMG.

"S'fine," the gorgeous stranger grumbled. He was super handsome, and his grin had her tummy doing somersaults as he flashed it her way. "You are mostly alone. Just me and a hungry shark."

"Shark?" Tracey screeched again, practically jumping on the man.

Thank goodness, she remembered herself before she did anything else humiliating. Nerves wracked her body, but one look in the man's crystalline gaze had her calming right down.

Holy cow. He is beautiful.

He really was the best looking man she had ever seen. Even better, he seemed to enjoy talking with her. Could she handle a little casual flirting? She wouldn't know if she didn't try.

Eeeeek!

After some minor discussion, she convinced the hunky man to turn around while she got out of the water. It took a second, but she pulled on her bathing suit and called out to him.

He'd stayed turned around the whole time—at

least she thought he had. And for some reason, that disappointed her.

Good manners are nice. Dirty boys are nicer, though.

Unfortunately, Tracey did not offer him the same courtesy. He strode from the water naked as the day he was born, *and holy freaking hotness,* the man was glorious.

She was dumbstruck as the man stepped out of the darkening waters, looking like a sea god about to embark on his reign over the dry lands.

He can reign over me anytime with that body. OMG. Did I just think that? I am a total slut.

She shook her head and dropped her gaze as he pulled on his trunks. What kind of person was she? Ogling a stranger—*not a stranger, his name is Phoenix Tala*—like he was some prize stallion was not becoming of a person with morals.

She should be ashamed of herself. Would be, too, as soon as she got the image of his perfect body out of her head. Which would be like two weeks from never. The man was packing some serious heat between his thick, rugby player thighs.

A person had to work out to have legs like that. Was he a professional athlete? It would not surprise her at all with his muscular build. Unfortunately, she knew fuck all about sports. Holy cow! Tracey was even cursing in her thoughts now.

"I should go," she mumbled.

"You wanna leave me, already? After all we've been through?" Phoenix replied and gave her a panty, *er*, swimsuit melting grin.

She was shocked at the easy banter that followed, and found herself agreeing to have dinner with the man. Phoenix caught her hand in his and sent her pulse racing with the simple gesture. Had anyone ever wanted to hold hands with her like that? She could not remember a time. He made her so nervous she couldn't even walk in a straight line.

"Sorry, I'm clumsy," she said, almost tripping once they got to the sidewalk. She was embarrassed and tried to laugh it off, stepping away from the man. But Phoenix held strong.

"You're not clumsy, Tracey."

"No, seriously, I am. And I'm so sorry about all this, roping you into dinner—"

"I was the one who asked you," he reminded her gently, and she warmed to him a little more.

"Why are you so nervous now? After a little tres-passing and skinny dipping, dinner should be no problem for a badass like you," Phoenix said.

"Me? I think you're getting a little ahead of yourself. I'm no badass. More like a short, chubby, stick in the mud, who still lives at home with her parents and never does anything for fun, or at least, I did up until a few hours ago," she admitted to her shock.

"Well, I don't know who you're talking about, but the Tracey I know—and yes, I consider myself an expert by now—is daring, courageous, beautiful as fuck, and has me completely captivated," Phoenix said, and damn, her stomach was doing somersaults at his praise.

Holy cow. The man's smile should be classified as a lethal weapon. Tracey tucked her damp hair behind her ear with her right hand, her left firmly encased in his. She licked her lips, cheeks were burning with embarrassment.

"Captivated, huh?" she asked.

"That's right. Now, I wanna get to know you, Tracey Donner."

"Why?"

"A hundred reasons, and yet, they all amount to the same thing."

"What's that?" she asked, wondering what kind of spell he was weaving around her to make her ask such questions aloud.

"I'll tell you," he said, clicking his tongue behind his teeth and looking slightly nervous for such a jaw-dropping gorgeous man. "After we eat, though. So, what do you like?"

"I like everything, obviously," she murmured.

"I don't know what you mean, why is it obvious?"

"Are you serious?"

"Yeah," he said, cocking his head to the side.

Holy crap, she could tell he was really serious. The man was not making a rude comment or joke about her weight, and she had no idea what to do with that information other than stand there in awe.

"Um, it's been pointed out to me before that I was overweight. So, when I said it was obvious, I eat everything, I guess I was being self-deprecating. Phoenix, I would like to apologize for that now—"

"You don't have a damn thing to apologize for, and anyone who ever made you feel less than is not worth a minute of your time, Tracey. Now, I like the way you look. Hell, I more than that, and if you need proof, well, I've been rocking a boner since I laid eyes on you. Now, I'm not telling you that to scare you," he continued, unrushed. "I have no intention of doing anything you don't want, you control the pace, I'm just throwing that out there, so there is no misunderstanding. I want you to know I find you incredibly hot."

"Wow. Well, first, thank you. That was quite the compliment," she said.

Tracey paused, casting a quick glance towards his swimsuit clad nether regions, and sure enough, the evidence of his admiration was right there, filling out his trunks with what had to be ten to eleven inches of long, hard man.

Yep, he's got a boner. And I gave it to him.

"But I wasn't apologizing for anyone else. I was apologizing because I should never have said anything like that. I'm turning a new leaf, Phoenix Tala, and you caught me right at the cusp."

"Really?"

"Yes, you see, I decided I like myself, curves, and quirks, and all. I won't be apologizing for myself anymore. And I am not looking for a man to save me or change me. Just thought you should know that up front."

It was the boldest statement Tracey had ever made, but she meant it. Sure, it was way too early for her to speak so plainly to the man, but maybe it would save her a little heartache to get it out in the open now. She stopped walking and looked into his face, expecting rejection and maybe even anger. Instead, Tracey was floored when she saw something closely resembling pride in his glittering green gaze.

"Good for you. Don't take anyone's shit, Tracey. Not ever. Least of all mine."

"You are the strangest man," she mused, and Phoenix tossed his head back and barked a loud laugh.

"Yeah," he murmured. "I get that sometimes. How about Mexican food?"

"I like Mexican," she replied as they fell into an easy rhythm side by side.

"So, what brings you to Maccon City?"

"Oh, well. That's a long, boring story," she replied, liking the feel of his warm hand around hers.

Rarely in life had Tracey ever felt small or dainty, but next to the behemoth of a man, she felt positively petite. The way he looked at her warmed her insides, and raw attraction flooded her system. It was pretty difficult to ignore the physical awareness blossoming between them. With his boner statement and all, it was a wonder she hadn't melted into a puddle of needy woman at his feet.

"I doubt any story about you could be boring," he returned.

"Why? You don't even know me," she stated, laughing a little at his bold reply.

Men didn't usually flirt with her. Especially not men who looked like him, so she couldn't be entirely sure that's what was happening.

"I'd like to get to know you, Tracey. Really, I would," he replied, taking care to look both ways before walking her across the street.

"Wow. So, you fake save me from a shark, get naked with me in the ocean, listen to part of my sob story, and you're still here, wanting more? I am not sure what you want from me, but you are wasting your time if you think I'm desperate enough to fall for a line like that," she said bluntly.

"It's no line," he growled, turning to face her. "I apologize if I offended you with my blunt talk earlier, but I meant everything I said. I want to spend time with you."

"You really do?"

"Yes."

"Okay, then. Let's get some Mexican food."

"Good," he said, and seemed to relax once more.

They started walking again, and she did her best to stay even with his long strides. Impossible really, since it took two of her shorter, less elegant steps to make one of his.

The man moved like a dancer. Or maybe a professional soccer player. All grace and understated power. No awkward stumbles or half steps for him. She couldn't imagine what it was like to be born with such innate dignity. He was really perhaps the most beautiful man she had ever seen.

Which begged the questions—what was he doing here? And why was he alone?

Sexy, puzzling man. I wonder what he's searching for.

With any luck, Tracey might find out.

CHAPTER 9

Gathering her courage, Tracey looked up at Phoenix, admiring his profile. She'd never gotten butterflies in her stomach just looking at a man—*except for when she saw Harry Styles in concert but come on—that was Harry Styles.*

Love him as she might, Harry had nothing on Phoenix Tala. His face was just as gorgeous, and his body, god-like.

"So, why are *you* in Maccon City?"

That brought both golden eyebrows up, and Tracey grinned. It was about time he got frazzled. But even more than the little bit of satisfaction she got from surprising the man, she really was curious.

"Well, I was itching for a road trip. So, I told my

Alph—*er*, I mean my boss, then I jumped on my bike and wound up here."

"Your bike? Wait—you have a motorcycle?" she asked, mouth gaping.

"Yeah. A Harley."

"OMG! Of course you do," she mumbled, rolling her eyes and shaking her head.

"What?" he asked.

"It just figures," she replied, and exhaled a laughing breath.

One of Tracey's most secret naughty girl fantasies involved a sexy stranger swooping in on a big badass motorcycle, wearing leather and denim. It was a hot dream. One that always made her motor run—*pun intended.*

Of course, skinny dipping with a sexy stranger was number two on her list of secret naughty girl fantasies. She'd thought she was one and done, but this hot boy had a Harley.

Swoon. Swoon. SWOON.

"Do you not like motorcycles?" Phoenix asked, looking down at her with concern in his glowing green gaze.

Sexy, sexy man.

His eyes were gorgeous. Sometimes they looked aquamarine wrapped in gold. Columbian emeralds, she mused. It must have been a trick of the light. But they were beautiful, stunning, like nothing else she'd ever seen.

"No."

"You don't?"

"No! Yes! I mean, I love motorcycles," she replied rapidly.

"I see." He grinned, beaming at her, and she thought he squeezed her hand a little longer that time.

"Well," she continued nervously. "I think I do. I've never actually been on a motorcycle before."

"I can rectify that. Just say when."

"Really?"

"Sure. Anytime you want. Hell, we can go right now."

Tracey stopped in her tracks. No man had ever offered to take her for a ride on his motorcycle before. Her mother would think it was undignified. Her father would consider it lowly.

But they weren't here right now. And even if they were, so what? Tracey was thirty, not thirteen. She did not need her parents' permission to do something wild—*like jumping on the back of a Harley with a complete stranger.*

"I'm sorry. Did I make you uncomfortable again?"

Phoenix frowned. He looked like he wanted to take back his invitation, but Tracey didn't want that. Her stomach was doing all kinds of somersaults, and she knew she was bound to make a fool of herself.

Bottom line, Tracey was finished living by other people's rules. Grabbing her courage, she shook her head at the gorgeous man.

"Okay, first, no, you did nothing wrong. I am actually surprisingly comfortable with you. Second, I would very much like to go for a ride on your Harley, but I have something to confess—"

"What?" he asked, looking completely enamored and making her tingle down to her toes.

"I'm starving. How about we have dinner first?"

"Sorry, I shouldn't have dallied," he murmured. "Let's get going."

He tugged on her hand gently, and Tracey felt like she was holding on to a live wire. Electricity zipped up and down her body, lighting her up like a neon sign from within. Pleasure hummed along her skin, like the breeze coming off the Atlantic. And all because of the almost impossible to believe knowledge that Tracey and Phoenix had this brand new, exciting, growing mutual attraction between them.

"You should know, I've never gone out with a guy

I just met," she stated, hoping against hope her brutal honesty wasn't about to cost her the night.

"No?"

"Nope. In fact, I don't have much dating experience at all."

"Well, I guess you and I can practice together."

He was grinning again, and she felt her heart skip a beat. She figured a guy who looked like that didn't chase women very often and imagined she was one in a long line of women who he'd asked out.

Crap.

What was she doing? He was gorgeous, and she was just her. Phoenix had to know the effect he had on women. Far too good-looking not to be aware of it.

OMG.

What if Rosa was right? What if he was some man who only went after rich women? Like a real live gigolo, wooing the first single woman he saw, and wanting her to pay for his lifestyle. He was certainly hot enough to be a kept playboy on the prowl.

No freaking way.

She was being an idiot. Tracey didn't believe that about Phoenix for a minute. Then again, what did she really know about him? Anything was possible, she supposed. If he was a kept man, his ridiculous hotness alone would command a pretty penny for the pleasure of his company.

"I'm sorry, I know this might sound rude, but are you by any chance a playboy?"

"A what?" Phoenix burst out, stopping in his tracks.

"Well, a friend of mine read about handsome men who come to places like this, like a beach resort, to prey on lonely, wealthy women. They get them to fall in love, or lust, and, *well*, they just love off them, I guess you could say. I'm not judging, I swear, but anyway, this friend planted this seed, and I thought it important to find out first. And, oh my God, I sound crazy. I will totally understand if you think I am nuts and want to call off dinner."

Crap. She was a nut job. He was so walking out on her. Why couldn't she just keep her big mouth shut?

Damn. Damn. DAMN.

"Uh, okay. First, thanks for the compliment. I mean, I think there was sort of a compliment in there about me being handsome," he replied, and he sounded like he was smiling, but Tracey couldn't tell. IN fact, she could not see his face at all since she was covering her eyes with her hands.

"Tracey, I am not a playboy, gigolo, or prostitute of any kind. Scout's honor," he teased.

"Oh my God! You're a boy scout? Now, I am really mortified," she squealed.

Deep, rich sounds of masculine laughter accompanied by large hands on her shoulders had her peeking out from behind her hands. God, he smelled good. A delicious combination of whatever spicy masculine cologne he wore and the fresh sea air.

"Tracey, it's okay," he said.

"Really, it's okay that I basically called you a-a—"

"A hooker?" he asked, and she slapped her hands over her mouth to cover up her squeak.

"OMG! I am so humiliated."

"Why? You know, I haven't been taken by surprise in a very long time. I think you are funny, smart, and so fucking adorable," he said kindly.

"I think you mean crazy, ridiculous, and not a good prospect at all," she replied, shaking her head.

"Nope. I said what I meant, beautiful."

Double swoon.

CHAPTER 10

Was there anything about this man that was unattractive? He was too good to be true.

"Phoenix Tala, are you some kind of angel walking on earth? I mean, you are just too good to be true."

"I'm no angel, Tracey."

"Well, you're not just a man either. You're too kind, too hot, and you even offered to take me for a ride on your bike after dinner."

"All my pleasure."

"How can you say that?"

"Easy. I get to be with you," he told her, and damn, her heart started pounding in earnest.

"This has been some day," she told him, exhaling as she tried to find her nerve.

Phoenix linked their hands again and pulled her through the sparse crowd. His shoulder brushed against hers, and tingles raced down her spine.

"How do you mean?" he asked once she was beside him again.

"For one thing, I ran away from home—yes, at my age, that is still possible. Then, I jumped in an Uber and traveled to Maccon City with no hotel reservations during peak season and almost wound up sleeping on the beach. Next, I went skinny dipping in the ocean with you, as it turned out. And now, here I am, insulting the sexiest man I ever saw and still getting him to take me to dinner."

"You've been busy, beautiful."

"Yeah, you can say that again. My whole life has gone upside down. Strangest. Day. Ever."

His glittering aquamarine eyes sparkled down at her, and she felt his attention down to her toes. He really seemed interested, and that, in itself, was amazing and awesome. Even more amazing, Tracey was enjoying herself. She'd embarrassed herself a dozen times or more, but he was still there, so maybe she was doing something right, after all.

"You know, if you want to talk about it, I'm here for you, beautiful."

"You really are too good to be true. Are you sure

someone didn't hire you to be nice to me?" She wondered aloud, biting her lip when his eyebrows furrowed in confusion.

"What? Woman, I don't know who you've been hanging with, but it is a privilege to be anywhere near you, and if it takes forever and a day, I'm gonna make it my job to make sure you believe that," Phoenix stated, narrowing his eyebrows.

Tracey stared, wide eyed. No one talked like that. At least not to her. Her pulse was racing as long-forgotten parts of her woke up with interest. When was the last time a man's gaze had made her feel so feminine and desired?

Never. Never ever ever.

But standing on the semi crowded sidewalk with this man, well, Tracey felt every bit the siren he seemed to think she was. It was a good feeling—*a very good feeling.*

Tracey did not want it to end. Could she trust it, though? That was the real question.

"Come on, beautiful, let's get some food and beer, or wine, if you prefer. We can chat or just enjoy the silence. Whatever you like."

"Okay, just answer me one question. Why did you ask me to go out to dinner with you?"

"Tracey, you seem to be operating under some

false belief that you aren't the most spectacular fucking thing I've ever seen. Let me clarify exactly how I feel about you right now."

He tugged on her hand, pulling her flush against his body. They were both still damp, smelling of sea salt and summer. Tracey's pulse raced, and even more amazing was the fact she could feel his own heartbeat pounding like a runaway train inside his chest. He dipped his head and brushed his lips against hers.

Holy crap.

The whisper of a kiss was so soft, so light, so full of promise—she felt it down to the soles of her bare feet. He brushed his mouth against hers, once, twice, and the third time, well, that really was the charm. He crushed his mouth to hers, one hand cupping her neck as he pushed past her semi-closed lips and delved inside her mouth with his long, hot tongue. Phoenix blew her mind with that kiss. She couldn't think or move. For several long seconds after he pulled away, Tracey remained breathing heavily. She still stood pressed against him, eyes half-closed, mouth throbbing from his passionate kiss.

"You believe me now?" he asked, his voice impossibly deep.

"Whoa."

"Yeah, whoa. If you hadn't agreed to come with me when I asked, I planned to ask you again tomorrow. And the day after that, and so on. I meant it, Tracey. I wanna get to know you," he said and brushed her hair back with his hands, dropping another soulful kiss onto her ready and waiting lips.

"Now, I know you're too good to be true," she whispered, and reached up on tiptoe to kiss him back quickly before she ran out of courage.

"Nope. Just honest. You got me wild for you, Tracey Donner," Phoenix growled against her mouth, deepening the kiss for a moment before pulling back.

She shook her head and tried to come up with something clever to say. There simply were not words for how she felt about this man.

"I think you are trying to seduce me," she blurted, half hopeful it was the truth.

His deep chuckle reached her ears, and Tracey blinked rapidly. Had she said that aloud?

Double crap.

The feel of his callused finger beneath her chin as he gently tilted her head upwards had her opening her eyes. Phoenix Tala was staring down at her from his incredible height, and damn, the man was potent this close.

Her whole body seemed to tremble and wait for him to do whatever it was he was about to do. She couldn't have made a bigger ass of herself if she'd tried, but he was still there. And God help her, Tracey wanted to know why.

"If it will help you to know what I am planning, beautiful, let me spell it out for you. First, I can hear your stomach growling, and I need to feed you—call it a biological imperative to see to your needs, if you like. Second, I plan to share that meal in your very delightful company. And third, I have every intention of seducing you, Tracey."

"What?"

"Come on, the restaurant is right here."

CHAPTER 11

Dinner. We are having dinner. Sure, I can do this. I can sit through dinner with my fated mate and pretend to be a normal for the night.

If he said it to himself enough times, maybe the urge to drag her to the floor and taste every inch of her would go away. His Wolf snarled, seeming to roll his eyes at him.

Yeah. Sure. Moron.

Phoenix waged war with his carnal desires as he guided the sexy female to an outdoor table inside an enclosed section of sidewalk just a few streets down from their hotel. The place claimed authentic Mexican cuisine, boasting fresh seafood and local ingredients.

Even better, they didn't have to waste time going

back to change. Tracey had a pretty, soft-looking blouse she'd pulled out of her bag and threw on over her bathing suit. It went with the sarong she had wrapped around her waist. The whole ensemble was hell on his nerves, with little sheer strips revealing tantalizing glimpses of skin—*like it was playing peek-aboo with him.*

Grrrr.

She looked gorgeous with her golden hair flowing in the breeze, and those creamy jade eyes of hers staring up at him all full of secrets and laughter. She was an enigma. A mysterious little beauty, and he could not wait to get to know her better. After their rocky start, and those tempting kisses that left him wanting more, having dinner should be a piece of cake.

Famous. Last. Words.

Phoenix's Dire Wolf was determined to claim the female tonight, and it was all he could do to talk the beast down. But it was all coming together so quickly. The delicious scent of her arousal told him she was interested, but she was a *normal.* A somewhat shy and sheltered normal at that. She would not understand what being fated mates to each other meant.

No. He had to slow it down. It was difficult,

though. Being with her was just so easy. She might be shy about her appeal, but she was downright bawdy with her humor and stories. Phoenix loved it.

He'd never been big on conversation, trusting computers more easily than people. But Tracey was different. She was exciting and alluring. He hadn't broached the subject of relationships yet. He was enjoying himself too much for reality to set in.

"Can I take your order?" the server asked, and Tracey turned a brilliant smile at the man that had Phoenix wanting to claw the fucker's eyes out.

Easy.

He hardly caught what she'd ordered, but knew from the amount of time it took, it was not nearly enough.

"For you, sir?"

"Can you double what she asked for? Great. Then add twenty chipotle wings, well done. An order of your famous "trash can" nachos with habanero mango salsa. Fresh guacamole. Oh, and six *birria* tacos, please."

"Um, yes, sir. Anything to drink?" the server asked.

Phoenix really loved a good tequila when he was enjoying Mexican cuisine. He looked at Tracey, catching her staring at him wide-eyed.

"Wanna split a pitcher of mango margaritas with me?"

"I shouldn't," she replied. "But that sounds wonderful."

"Excellent," the server replied and hurried off to put their order in.

A few minutes later, he came back with a frosty pitcher of mango margs, a couple of waters, and some appetizers. Phoenix grinned, and served Tracey before himself, laughing when she appeared stunned at the amount of food he'd ordered.

"Did you invite like six other people to dinner with us?"

"No, are you fat shaming me?" he teased.

"Hardly," Tracey replied, taking a guacamole filled tortilla chip right out of his hand and another from his dish.

"This is so good, but you need to try it this way," she told him, smiling vibrantly, and damn, if this woman didn't light up like a star when she was happy.

Phoenix loved watching her. She was full of surprises and hidden depth. She lifted a spoon, proceeding to do about the most amazing thing he had ever seen. While chewing the chip she'd stolen from him, she prepared another with just a smidge of guacamole and mango habanero salsa before leaning over and offering it to him.

"This is the perfect chip," she whispered, eyes wide, as if she only realized the intimacy of what she was doing.

Hell if he was going to let her balk now. Phoenix took the proffered bite, nibbling her fingertips gently and moaning appreciatively. She was right. Perfect bite, indeed.

That little offering of hers sealed it. This sexy normal was definitely his mate. Phoenix could not remember the last time he'd shared food with anyone. But here he was, in public, taking nibbles from her hand like a puppy with its new master.

Grrrr.

The Wolf didn't necessarily like the comparison, but that was too fucking bad. Even his beast recognized her as his. He could have crowed, he was so dang happy. For too long, Phoenix had thought he was broken. He figured he was too rough for a woman, a nomadic creature like him. Then Derrick made them put down roots, and he'd been at sea.

"Ooh, try this," Tracey interrupted his thoughts, snagging the chip he'd almost gotten all the way to his mouth and adding some shredded jalapenos and lime juice with some Mexican table cream on top.

Phoenix opened like a good boy, loving the fact that she was feeding him and talking animatedly. Last time Weylin tried to snag a chip from his plate, Phoenix had wrestled the bastard to the ground, and they'd bled all over the kitchen floor at the Pack house.

His inner beast was territorial about food. But his Wolf didn't seem to mind Tracey taking from his plate. Not at all.

"Everything tastes so good," she moaned around a mouth full of shrimp ceviche.

Fucking hell.

The woman was downright noisy when she ate. Moaning in delight over the tasty goodies. Brock's mate, Ariella, was notorious for her eating noises, but damn, Tracey could sure give the Lioness a run for her money.

"Here you go," the server returned, interrupting Phoenix's train of thought.

He swapped out empty plates, and food they were finished with for new, full dishes with their entrees. Phoenix had doubled her order and added more to it. As if the man knew how much Phoenix enjoyed sharing with her, the server had set it all up on platters, bringing two empty plates for them to share.

The next hour went by unrushed, and the more she relaxed, the happier his Wolf was. She was perfect. He frowned, worrying over her reaction to his secret. Would she run? Fuck, he didn't know if she could survive it. The more time he spent in her company, the more his Wolf bonded to her, and Tracey was quickly becoming hella important to his very survival.

Mine.

"I know you're this big, beefy guy, but I can't believe how much you eat," Tracey said, laughing as Phoenix put away his eighth taco.

"I'm dainty as fuck," he joked, offering her the last bite of his *birria* taco.

"I can't, I'm stuffed."

"Interesting word, beautiful," he growled, winking to ensure she caught the innuendo.

"OMG. You did not just say that to me," she replied, and snorted behind her hand. "OMG. I snorted! Real attractive."

"I sure think so. Here, let's order dessert next," he whispered, taking her hand in his as the server cleared the dishes.

A few minutes later, the man returned with a tower of dessert nachos doused in cinnamon sugar, drizzled with chocolate sauce and caramel, and topped with sliced berries and vanilla bean ice cream.

"You're trying to kill me," she moaned, eyes huge as she stared at the delicious confection.

"Never. You are one hundred percent safe with me, beautiful. Now, it's my turn to feed you," he murmured, taking a chip and adding a bit of this and that from the plate.

He growled softly as Tracey opened her mouth, allowing him to place the dessert in her mouth. She chewed and swallowed it down with a satisfying hum that made his dick hard in his shorts.

The fact she trusted him to feed her was deeply rewarding to both him and his Dire Wolf. The beast inside longed to chase the bite of dessert with a deep, soulful kiss, but he didn't think he could stop there. It would have to wait.

Patience is a virtue. Grrrr.

He wasn't known for his patience. But being there with her was almost enough to fulfill him. She was so open and positively bubbling with sweetness and hidden depths.

"Do you like art?" Tracey asked.

"I do," Phoenix replied with a warm smile. "Though I admit folk art is my favorite. I spent a couple of months in my youth just biking through

South America. I visited ancient ruins, rainforests, cities, and quaint little villages where the local men and women wove the most amazing rugs and tapestries, ponchos, blankets, you name it. I keep one I got in Ecuador in my bedroll on my bike."

"Really? That is amazing," she replied, and he heard the truth in her voice.

Her eyes lit up as she spoke, and he wanted to keep that light there. He wanted to make her happy and excited, always. Wondered how she would glow for him once he got his hands on her. Would she be noisy like when she liked something she ate? Would she give him one of those heart-stopping smiles he coveted from her?

Oh, the things he was going to do to and for his sweet mate. What did she like? How would she taste? The questions were rolling through him like a freight train, and he had to fight for control as his baser instincts pushed to the forefront. He should have known better than to think he could take things slowly. The physical pull to his mate was undeniable.

Shit.

She was saying something, and he was gonna fuck himself up if he missed even a single word of it. Tracey was that special to him already. He never wanted to be absent for a moment of the time he spent with her.

"I'd love to go there," she said, and her eyes took on a wistful glow as she spoke. "I've always wanted to travel. I mean, I went away with my family, but it was always stuffy hotels and scheduled trips to museums and things like that with groups or nannies."

"I see. Well, was it all bad?"

She paused and seemed to consider the question. Curiosity piqued, Phoenix realized he was truly interested in her reply. He wanted to know more about her. No, he didn't like her sadness, but he wanted to know everything.

The good. The bad. All of it. All of her.

He would take it inside, make it part of him, and learn how to please and care for her based on her past. Already, he made plans inside his head to take her on a trip to see the folk art of countries like Columbia, Peru, and Ecuador. Hell, he'd take her anywhere she wanted.

I'd do anything for her. Anything at all.

Mine.

"Not all of it, no. It was nice sometimes. My parents aren't bad. We're just different. I mean, I did kinda run away from home to come here."

"You waited a little while to run away. How come?"

"Stupid. Scared. A combination of both maybe?"

Her soft derisive snort almost missed his sensitive ears, but he caught it and frowned as she sipped from her glass of water. They'd finished the pitcher of margaritas and switched to water halfway through the meal.

Other dates he'd been on with women usually ended with him having to do the ordering and choosing, but he liked this so much better. Tracey knew her own mind and her likes and dislikes. She ate and drank what she wanted with no pressure or leaving it up to him or anyone else.

She thought she was a coward, but he knew different. Tracey was a motherfucking superstar, kicking ass and taking names.

"I don't believe that for a second. Weren't you the badass stripping down to her skin on private property and jumping into shark-infested waters?"

"Ha! Yeah, right. Thank you for that though," she replied and giggled.

"Nothing that isn't true, beautiful."

"I'm sorry, I don't want to put a damper on our evening so, let's just say I have never really gotten along with my mother. Besides, I am thirty years old.

I don't need permission to go to the beach if I want to."

"I don't suppose you do," he returned.

"This was nice," she said as he paid the bill at his insistence.

"It's only day one, Tracey. I plan on showing you a lot more nights like this," he promised.

She had no idea what she was in for, and Phoenix could not wait to show her.

CHAPTER 12

Tracey woke up the next morning with her heart pounding a steady tattoo in her chest. Her dreams were feverish, dirty, erotic—all the above. And they featured one man. Phoenix Tala.

The gorgeous, *not a stranger anymore*, hottie had walked her to her door after dinner and dessert, which, ironically, happened to be next door to his own room at the *Oasis*.

Oh, she'd wanted more than the delicious kiss he'd given her, but Tracey was new to this sort of thing. Insecurities had threatened to send her packing, but the big, beautiful man shook his head and grabbed her chin, stealing one last, deep kiss before forcing himself away.

He liked her. She felt it to her bones. And

dammit, she liked him too. It was way too soon for these feelings, but Tracey had never been good at playing games and waiting. Another thing her mother and her rich friends made fun of her for. But Tracey could not care less about them.

He kissed me.

Her skin buzzed with anticipation as she showered and dressed. Phoenix had asked her to spend the day with him, and she couldn't wait to start.

"Oh my, who is it?" Tracey asked when someone knocked at the door.

She'd just pulled on a floral printed sundress and was still scrunching her hair when she pulled it open. There he was, looking tempting and hot with the sunshine lighting him up from behind.

"Good morning, beautiful." Phoenix smiled, handing her a to go cup of coffee from the posh place down the street.

"Thanks," she replied, taking it from him. "I really need this."

"I know. You said so last night," he replied with a sexy chuckle.

Last night was the best date Tracey ever had. It was the first time in memory that a man hadn't mentioned her weight or eating habits, and she had actually enjoyed herself. Thoroughly.

About damn time, girl.

"Ready? I have some plans for us today," he told her, and his grin was infectious.

"Well then, let's get started," she replied, taking his offered hand.

That was another something new. Phoenix couldn't seem to help it. It was like he enjoyed touching her, and wasn't that new? Even better, she liked it, too.

Last night he'd held her hand when they walked, and at dinner, he seemed to find excuses to brush her fingertips or touch her shoulder or leg while they ate. And not in a grabby pervy way, either. He made her feel special—*pretty, too.*

Tracey liked those feelings. A lot. The man was weaving some sort of spell around her, and as she closed her room door, her coffee in one hand, his hand in the other, she wondered if he knew it.

"Do you believe in magic?" she asked out of the blue.

"Yes," he replied instantly. "Why?"

"You'll think it's silly," she murmured, walking down the stairs to the street with him beside her.

"I won't. Promise," he said, nudging her shoulder and squeezing her fingers carefully.

He stopped walking, and she was forced to stop,

too. Her eyes met his, reluctantly, jade green to glittering Columbian emeralds. Damn, he was beautiful. Like some hero from a book. She might as well get this over with. He would probably laugh it off, anyway.

Find your backbone, Tracey. You got this.

"Talk to me, beautiful," he whispered, and she relaxed.

He was the only man who'd repeatedly called her that, and her heart melted a little more with every utterance of the word. With Phoenix, Tracey felt beautiful. Even more so, she felt confident, and that was a good feeling. One everyone deserved to experience.

"It's just, I feel like this whole thing, you and me meeting in this place, is kismet," she whispered, eyes widening as heat seemed to fill her.

Phoenix moved closer, brushing her body with his as he let go of her hand and moved it to her neck. He'd already tossed his coffee cup into the trash can at the foot of the stairs. Both hands were on her now and as his head lowered and he nuzzled her lips with his own, Tracey gasped. Sizzling zaps of electricity raced up her spine, and she swayed on her feet, needing him to kiss her more firmly.

"Me too, Tracey. I feel it, too."

Then he kissed her, hard and deep, tasting of coffee and man. The combination was delicious, and she loved every second of it. Too soon, he ended the kiss, and they continued down the street with him holding her hand.

They grabbed some Jersey shore breakfast sandwiches—pork roll, fried egg, and cheese on a roll with salt, pepper, and ketchup. Delicious.

After they'd eaten, they headed for the beach. Phoenix had a cabana all booked for them, and she was glad she wore a bathing suit beneath her sundress.

They spent the afternoon swimming, and talking, sharing tidbits of information about each other. She learned his likes and dislikes, discussed movies, books, and random pop culture factoids.

He was so interesting, and he seemed eager to get to know her better. They were treading water, enjoying the low tide, and Tracey was so focused on his answer to her latest question, she didn't see the wave sneaking up on her. Phoenix's head shot up.

"Tracey, watch out!" he yelled.

Before she could blink, he swam half a dozen feet of water and pulled her beneath the rough wave, keeping her safe in his steel embrace. She clung to him as the wave passed over them, gasping for breath when he dragged her up.

"Are you, alright?" he asked, hands going over her worriedly.

She was sputtering for air, but nodding her head as she took in the scene around her. Other swimmers had been knocked sideways, and lifeguards were blowing whistles and helping bathers get their bearings. The Atlantic Ocean was infamous for sudden changes in roughness, and soon things had returned to calm.

"Let's get out a while, okay?" he suggested, and she nodded, still trying to find her air.

"Phoenix?"

"Yeah?" he asked, grabbing a huge beach towel and wrapping it around her shoulders as he helped her sit in one of their rented chairs.

"How did you do that?"

"How did I do what?" he replied, but he wouldn't meet her eyes, and was busying himself grabbing waters from the cooler.

"You practically blurred across the water to reach me."

"I'm just a fast swimmer, I guess."

But that was not entirely true. She hated he was not giving her a real answer, but she took the offered bottle, watching closely as relief crossed his face when she took a sip.

"I'll accept that answer for now, Phoenix Tala. But I know you are keeping something from me. Secrets are never fun and always discovered," she murmured.

"I promise I will tell you everything you want to know, it's just, let's just have today."

"What do you mean?"

"I mean, I don't want you running from me before you get to know me," he confessed, kneeling in front of her and rubbing her towel covered arms.

He looked haunted and unsure. It was the first time she'd seen the man look anything other than confident. It rattled her, but Tracey wasn't willing to end her time with him over some vague response to what was probably a trick of the mind.

"Hey, you're growling," she whispered, placing her hand on his chest.

Phoenix trembled under her touch. His aquamarine eyes were wide with some unspoken emotion, but before she could question it, he sat back, leaving her hand hovering in the air, and ran a hand over his face.

Trouble. The man was trouble.

If she was not careful, Tracey was going to lose

her heart to this man with so many secrets. She could be patient if she wanted to be, and for some reason, she did. This all felt too right to dismiss. He felt right to her.

"You okay now?" he asked.

"Yes, much better. But I think I'm done with the beach for the day," she replied, and smiled.

"Alright. Come on, let's go change for the rest of our adventure day."

Phoenix stood up and pulled her up with him. He tossed some bills at the rental station, taking her hand as he led her off the sand.

She went with him easily, but her curiosity warred with her need for caution. It was a sour note on the otherwise perfectly delightful day. Tracey hated the distance between them after that wave incident. She should have zipped her lip, but she could not go back to being the scared girl taking whatever crumbs of affection the people in her life offered her.

If Phoenix wanted to be in her life. He was going to have to give her more. She deserved that.

CHAPTER 13

Tracey hummed as she stripped off her swimsuit and stepped inside the shower. Two days had passed since she first swam into Phoenix's hot and naked body in the cool Atlantic waters. Two days of adventures and dates, steamy kisses, and endless conversations.

She'd had more fun in his company than she ever had with anyone else before. He took her swimming, bicycling, and hiking. They'd gone out for every meal, sometimes picnicking it on the beach. The man loved to eat, and he was always encouraging her to try things and steal bites from his plate. Last night, they'd gone to the pier and rode the amusement rides and played boardwalk games.

She felt like a teenager with her first crush. But it was more than that. Phoenix was quickly consuming her every waking thought. For the first time, her body stirred at the mere thought of a man.

She'd never been overly sexual. In fact, one of the few times she'd tried sex, her partner had called her cold and unfeeling. That remark had hurt Tracey for years. But maybe the fault wasn't with her because sure as the sun was shining right now, Tracey felt anything but cold with Phoenix.

No, they hadn't had sex yet, but she wanted to. Last night they were so close. They'd stayed up till dawn, making out like horny teenagers and talking like old friends.

Phoenix had walked her to the hotel room door last night and kissed her again, and again, and again, leaving her wanting before rushing off to his room right next door.

They hardly ever stayed just at the hotel, but this morning they'd shared breakfast, creamed chipped beef on enormous buttermilk waffles and fruit salad, on one of the poolside picnic tables on the lower level. After that, they swam and hung out, enjoying the amenities at the Oasis.

They spent the day swimming and playing in the pool like kids. Then they'd gone across the street to the beach. Tracey had never felt so uninhibited and free.

Her skin was soft bronze from her time in the sun, but he was even darker. For a blond, the man had tanned nicely, and his skin had a natural bronze glow, people paid good money to replicate, without that burned orange look so many sported. Tracey had never been so sun-kissed before.

They'd had lunch by the water and talked for what seemed like hours, but he didn't act bored with her. There was more to Phoenix Tala than met the eye.

"You work with computers?" she'd asked.

"Sometimes, yes. I have many interests, but I am also the partial owner of a roadhouse in Blue Valley."

"Really? What's it called?"

"Serious Moonlight."

"I heard of that! That is so cool. Who are your partners?"

"My Pa—my friends," he'd replied, strangely. "How about you?"

"Well, so far, I've done very little. I went to college, had a couple of jobs I didn't like."

"Doesn't sound little to me. What is it you want to do with your life, beautiful?"

No one had ever asked her that before, but the answer seemed to matter. So, she told him the truth.

"Truth is, I've always wanted to open my own store. I want to design bags. My parents would hate it, of course, but I've been making them for a few friends and myself over the years. I made this one," she'd confessed.

Tracey had picked up the large tote bag she'd designed and decorated with a mosaic of fabric tiles into the shape of a wolf howling at the moon. It was one of several pieces she'd made for herself, and a favorite of hers. She loved wolves. There was just something so wild and free about the beautiful creatures.

"That is beautiful. I didn't know you were an artist."

His eyes had zeroed in on the gold-outlined wolf she'd created out of different fabrics, and she'd felt her cheeks go warm at his praise.

Surprising, dangerous, sexy man.

Her time spent with Phoenix had been wonderful. Only one thing marred it—the secrets he kept from her. She'd felt it, that distance he worked so hard to keep hidden. It hurt her knowing she shared bits of her soul with him, but he wasn't willing to do the same.

Coupled with the way the sexy hottie kept

halting their physical relationship, to her unending frustration, Tracey was losing her mind. Of course, in the light of day, she understood she should appreciate his restraint.

Sex wasn't easy for Tracey. She'd only been with two men, and both had been longtime boyfriends before she'd slept with them. But appreciation was the farthest thing from her mind.

Her entire body was screaming for her to jump the big, sexy man. She was so done with the light petting and deep kisses. Tonight, she was determined to shake him up. With a little luck and some seduction, she was hoping to make this vacation fling into something more. But wanting to be with him, was not the same thing as being able to handle a one night stand with the man.

If only I was a casual sex kinda girl.

Wasn't his fault she was falling for him, or was it? He was intelligent and funny, and genuinely interested in her as far as she could tell. He seemed so tender and attentive to her needs. Being with him felt right. It felt huge. He was important. And call her crazy, but Tracey believed he felt the same way.

Was she wrong about his feelings? Only one way to find out. Finding the courage to ask was going to take everything she had, but Tracey had to know if the man she was falling for wanted her too.

Tonight, Phoenix was going to take her for a ride on his Harley. Tracey was nervous and excited. She'd always fantasized about riding behind a big sexy ass man on a motorcycle and now was her chance. She was more than ready. She'd had enough of stuffy and stodgy in her life.

No, thank you.

Tracey wanted wild and free and fun. Phoenix was all that, and so much more. The man with the aquamarine eyes was surprisingly deep. She was curious about him, what made him tick, what he liked, what he saw in her.

She loved the way he watched her. Like she was something worth seeing. Oh, and the way he was always touching her made the butterflies in her stomach turn into turbo jets.

She'd made one phone call to Rosa in all that time. The woman seemed so happy to hear from her, but when she'd asked about her parents, it was more of the same. The Donners were angry she didn't make their party, and her mother expressed said anger by leaving their Fairfield mansion and charting a yacht for the remainder of the season.

Guess you really miss me, Mother.

She tried not to let the sting hurt her. Her parents had chosen their lives, and now it was time for their daughter to do the same. And Tracey Donner was determined to have a life of her choosing.

It was fast, for sure, only a few days since she'd first bumped into him, but Tracey was positive Phoenix was going to be part of her life. She felt things she'd never imagined with the man. The phone rang, and she landed belly first on the bed to grab it.

"Hello?" she said breathlessly.

"Hey, beautiful. Look, I am heading out to gas up the bike, but I'll be back in a few minutes. You almost ready?" Phoenix asked, and she could almost see his panty-melting grin through the line.

It gave her chills. Her heart seemed to want to beat out of its cavity whenever he came near her.

"Perfect. Yeah, I'll probably need about fifteen or twenty minutes," she guessed.

"You got 'em, beautiful. I'll come to your door to get you when I'm finished."

"Alright. See you soon," she replied, hanging up and gasping.

God, he was so romantic. Always walking her to and from her door. Those first worries she had about him being out of her league seemed to lessen every day. He made her feel cared for, protected, and desired.

That afternoon, a tall, skinny, bikini-clad woman had tossed a frisbee in the direction of the blanket she was sharing with Phoenix, and Tracey's stomach had clenched. The woman was clearly flirting, but he didn't even blink. He just caught the bit of plastic before it could collide with Tracey's face and tossed it back straightaway.

Sexy, hot man.

Tracey could never compete with the model skinny woman, but with him, there did not seem to be a competition. Sure, she was all curves and chub, while the other woman was lithe and lean, but Phoenix seemed to prefer her.

The way he looked at Tracey made her blood boil. Another reason she was being extra careful with her appearance tonight. She wanted to give him her very best efforts. He was more than worth it, and so was she.

Tracey left her hair down, the way he liked it, and she slipped on another sundress she'd bought at one of the boardwalk stores. It had purple flowers on it and hugged her curves just right. She applied dark mascara with smokey eyeliner to her jade eyes, bringing out the creamy green color, and she added a tinted cherry red lip gloss to her lips.

Tracey worried her lower lips as she slipped a pair of slinky boy shorts beneath her dress. The undergarment was barely there, but it held her in and would hide her butt while she rode on the back of his bike.

She finished the look with a pair of comfortable flats. She felt good about herself in this outfit. Young and pretty. Flirty, too.

Outfit complete, she waited impatiently for seven to roll around. She had a few minutes left until he got back and decided to wait by the rooftop pool.

It was so pretty up there, and the view of the ocean was incomparable. Tracey exited her room, grabbing her bag and key. She wasn't paying attention to where she was walking when she tripped over something hard and furry.

"Ooof," she grunted as her knees collided with the slip-proof floor tiles.

Before the familiar feeling of humiliation at her own clumsiness could rise, Tracey blinked at the object that had tripped her.

"Tracey! Are you okay?" she heard someone call her name, but it was too late.

"Excuse me, I—" Tracey faltered, eyes glued to the enormous striped beast in front of her, she scrambled back, covering her mouth with her hand.

"Oh my God! It's a *tttiiiigggerrr!*"

She screamed, right before she passed out.

CHAPTER 14

"I'm sorry! I didn't mean to do it!"

Dean Jr. wailed as he clung to his mother's knees, naked as the day he was born. Phoenix patted the cub on his head, pacing as the doctors looked his mate over.

"I know, baby. It's okay. The nice lady will wake up real soon," Violet Romero, the cub's mother, cooed in a pleasing voice.

Unfortunately, the boy's father, Dean Romero, Neta of the Island Stripe Pride, was not as easily appeased. He growled at Phoenix with the force of his beast, irritating the fuck out of his inner Dire Wolf.

"A human? You brought a *human* here? What the *fudge*, man," he spat the non-curse word with as much ferocity as if he'd dropped the f-bomb in front of his son.

"I am sorry. I expected to have told her by now. NO disrespect intended, Mr. Romero. And, yes, Tracey is a normal, just as your Nari once was."

Phoenix tried reasoning with the man. After all, Violet was a human before she'd been claimed by the Tiger king.

"That is irrelevant. She could out us all, man. There are laws for a reason," Dean retorted.

"She is my mate, Neta. And I am not of your Pride. Please, do not try to use your Alpha voice on me. It just pisses my Wolf off."

Phoenix spoke in an even voice, trying hard to keep control of his beast. It happened now and again where a Shifter would try to challenge his prehistoric monster of a creature. Usually, the result was a gory mess of epic proportions. He really, really did not want to go there.

"Sorry. I am protective of my family, and the woman startled my cub," Dean hissed, running a hand over his face. "Look, I've heard of your kind. Dire Wolves are tough, secret creatures and my Tiger can feel your dominance. It is making me anxious. Truly, I have no quarrel with you. I have enough to keep me busy with my Pride and my family," he explained.

"I get that. NO worries. I am not here to challenge you. I was just trying to take it slow," Phoenix explained, cursing himself ten times the fool for the bad way he'd handled this whole thing.

His animal had chosen her the moment he saw her. The Fates had brought them together, yes, but it was his human side falling in love with the beautiful woman. More and more with every second that passed.

"So, she is yours?" The Tiger king asked.

Phoenix nodded. He applauded the man's efforts to rein in his own dominant as fuck cat. It was not easy, being a monster.

"Yes," he said, his voice full of his Dire Wolf as he gazed upon Tracey's still unconscious form, where he placed her on her bed.

The animal was not fucking happy. Not at all. His beast snarled and scratched inside of him, but he kept his skin. Phoenix refused to allow his Wolf to master him. After all, the child was not to blame, and Dean had a point. He should have explained things to her as soon as he knew she was his.

Fucking hell.

"Dean, take it easy. Our cub is fine, and she is his

mate. Naturally, he is trying to take things slowly," Violet said to her husband. "I'm going to take Junior back to our room for a bath to get him settled down. Good luck, Phoenix. I hope for the best," she replied kindly.

She kissed her mate on the cheek and offered Phoenix a small smile. The cub turned his big eyes on him, and his Wolf relaxed, allowing him to smile for the child.

He had no quarrels with cubs. The boy was just doing what boys did. Besides, this rooftop was his playground. A Shifter-only floor at the hotel, where the rest of the human guests were off-limits.

"I am sorry, little one, if my mate scared you." Phoenix told the cub in a gentle voice.

"S'okay mister. But she's gonna be really mad at you. Daddy buys Mama flowers when he makes her mad. Maybe you should try that?"

"Thanks for the advice, sport. I will take it into consideration."

He grinned at the tyke and nodded. It was sound advice, after all.

"Okay, we will leave you to it," Dean said, smiling at his boy. "Oh, and uh, I'll intercede with Rafe Maccon. I will explain the situation since he's already been apprised by the guards here,"

Dean said, surprising Phoenix with his generosity.

"I appreciate it, Neta."

Phoenix bowed his head slightly in reverence to the man's position. His Dire Wolf would not allow him to submit to anyone but his own Alpha, but the beast was not interested in asserting his dominance at the moment.

No. He was far more concerned with how to approach the precarious situation he found himself in. The Pride doctor came out of the room, explaining she was fine, just in shock.

The moon was low in the sky and a thousand stars sparkled above them. It was beautiful, but nothing compared to his sweet mate. He watched as her chest rose and fell with every breath. The tempting little dress she wore revealed her petal soft skin and stirred him like no one else ever could.

Tracey moaned, creamy green eyes blinking slowly as she came to. A smile teased the corner of her bow of a mouth and Phoenix dropped a soft kiss there, unable to stop himself.

She was all things tempting and tasty. His own personal beauty. A sultry seductress who could bring him to his knees without even trying. And the incredible female did not even know it.

"Phoenix, what happened? How did I get back in my room?" Tracey asked, and sat up slowly.

He noticed the very moment she remembered. Fear and curiosity seemed to war within her. Eyes wide, she scrambled up and out of the bed.

"There was a tiger outside my room. I tripped over him. W-what? How? I think, uh, I'm losing my mind," she said and covered her eyes.

"Hey now, sweetheart, come here. Let me explain."

"Explain what? How I'm going crazy?" She shook her head, near hysterics.

He hated she was so upset. Knowing he was to blame didn't comfort him. But he was a man, a Dire Wolf, and he would do what he must in order to bring any degree of peace to his mate's mind. He took her hand and tugged her close, wrapping her in a tight embrace.

Her ready submission to his touch unnerved him. Fuck, she was so trusting and sweet. Generous with herself in ways he had never imagined possible.

"I'm so sorry, love. This is all my fault. I should have explained better."

"Explained? How can you explain my delusions?"

"Tracey, you are not delusional," he said, cupping her face gently in his hands.

"Phoenix?"

"What you saw was real, and it's all part of the secret I've been keeping from you."

"What? Are you part of some underground exotic pet ring or something?" she asked, confused.

"No, of course not. The cub you saw was a Tiger Shifter."

"A what?"

"A Shifter. Like a Werewolf, but different. This hotel is owned and operated by Shifters, and they specifically cater to families. This rooftop is supposed to be a haven for those families to be who they are naturally, without fear or consequence. When I told Marco to give you a room up here, it was because I knew the moment I saw you, you were mine."

"What are you talking about?"

Phoenix exhaled a breath and tried to find the right words. He was fucking this up.

"They were out of regular rooms, and I had to beg Marco to allow you to stay here. I told him I would tell you immediately what we were to each other, but I did not want you to run, Tracey. I waited. It was a mistake, and I am very sorry," he told her.

"You aren't making any sense, Phoenix."

"*I* am a *Shifter*, Tracey."

"What? You're a Tiger?"

"Huh? No. I'm a Wolf. A Dire Wolf, actually, and you are my fated mate. Supernaturals exist in the world, under the radar of the human world. We have since the beginning of time," he explained.

"Are you making fun of me?" she asked in a small voice, and he hated he made her doubt herself.

"Never," he told her earnestly. "Shifters and other supernaturals are very real. Part of our connection to the universe is an understanding with the Fates, who we believe have selected our mates before our births. You are my fated mate, Tracey Donner. I knew it the second I saw you."

"You're saying impossible things," she whispered, tears welling in her beautiful eyes.

Fuck. He looked at her for the first time tonight and was stunned. Tracey was a knockout anyway, but tonight she'd put more effort into her appearance. The smoky accents around her eyes made their color so much more intense. She was so beautiful, he could hardly breathe.

"No. Not impossible, beautiful," he told her, cupping his hand around her neck. Thank fuck, she did not flinch from him.

"I should have told you right away. But I wanted to wait until you got to know me better."

"Phoenix, I confess I thought you were too good to be true since day one," she began, and this time, she did pull away from him. "Now it makes sense. You're delusional, too!"

"No! No, I'm not delusional, and neither are you," he growled impatiently.

Shit.

"Great. Just great. You're the first guy I've considered sleeping with in like a year and you're batshit crazy. I think I liked it better when I thought you were a male prostitute," Tracey muttered and shook her head, wiping the stray tears that rolled down her cheeks.

"I never should have left Fairfield. My mother was right, I'm a mess. I have to go."

"Tracey! Wait! I will prove it to you."

"You know, I poured my heart out to you. How could you do this?"

"Do what? I am just trying to talk to you," he tried again, but her mixed emotions and reactions were wreaking havoc with him.

Her myriad of feelings was egging his Wolf on to a near fucking panic. And that was so not good. The beast was wild to calm her down, to do anything to make her feel better.

"You don't have to pull this kind of stunt to get me to leave you alone. Making fun of me is not okay," she replied, and her misery was so clear it gutted him.

"What are you talking about? I don't want you to leave me alone, Tracey. I can't live without you!" He roared.

Shit.

He was really losing it. Fear, unlike anything he ever felt, gripped him as she walked away. He could not let her go. Not until he got her to listen! That he caused her fear and pain was nauseating. Phoenix would never hurt her.

Fucking hell.

He would chew off his own paw before he did that. But it looked like he had without trying. He wanted to hunt down every single person in her life who made her doubt herself.

All of those ingrates who'd savaged her pride and esteem that she would believe herself unworthy of his affection or attentions. Those people did not deserve to know her. But what now? She thought he was playing games.

Fuck. Fuck. FUCK!

"Wait!"

"What? What is it you want? To make up some more crazy stories?" She turned and yelled back, causing his own eyes to widen and lips to quirk.

Holy shit.

His Wolf growled appreciatively when he saw what was really in her eyes. Tracey wasn't afraid of him. His mate was royally fucking pissed.

Joy spread through him like wildfire at the prospect of his sexy little mate being madder than fuck at him. Her pain would eat him alive, but her anger? Well, that he could deal with.

"Want to know what I want?" he growled, stalking her until her back was up against the railing overlooking the sand.

"Yes. What do you want?" she asked, eyes flashing in the moonlight and chest heaving.

Fuck.

His dick was being strangled by the jeans he had on. He'd dressed for a ride, and was walking languidly to get her, trying to give her time to finish dressing.

He'd heard her screaming and cursed himself for wasting time, daydreaming about the night to come and what he had planned for them, when her panic slammed into him. He'd climbed the stairs three at a time and found her on the floor and the cub in tears.

Fucking denim had no give, and he was ready to burst just from being near her. He backed her up till she was stuck between him and the guardrail.

Phoenix slammed his hands down on either side of her, noting her sharp intake of breath and the heady scent of her lust that filled his nostrils. It was better than any other scent or drug he could ever have imagined. She was fucking dynamite—and like it or not she was his.

"What I want is you, Tracey. Only you," he growled, making sure she saw his Dire Wolf shining out through his gaze before claiming her mouth in a kiss neither of them would ever forget.

Mine.

His Dire Wolf howled in that metaphysical plane where he dwelled, waiting for Phoenix to call him forward. The sound pierced his eardrums till he thought he would never hear another thing in reality.

"Wait a minute," she grunted, pushing against his chest.

Phoenix loosened his hold. It would always be her choice to give him access to her body or not. He would never force any woman, much less his mate. Her needs and desires were everything to him.

"You said I'm yours. Does that mean you're mine?" she asked, and he nodded.

"This isn't just some game to you?"

"No games, Tracey. My Wolf has already bonded to you. We pick one, one mate, and I knew the moment I saw you what you were to me."

Watching her closely, he waited for her to decide, satisfaction humming through him as her eyes lit up like fire. Holy fuck, her creamy jade eyes seemed circled with orange red flames, and he growled deep in his chest. She was breathtaking.

One minute, she was watching him with those hypnotizing eyes, the next, Tracey grabbed the collar of his t-shirt and tugged him back down to her welcoming mouth. Tracey moaned and wrapped her arms tight around his neck, giving as good as she got, and Phoenix knew it would be okay.

Mine.

Thank fuck.

CHAPTER 15

What am I doing?

She moaned as Phoenix slipped his tongue past her lips and devoured her in a kiss so hot, it turned her knees to jelly.

Seems clear enough, Tracey. You are being kissed stupid by a man who claims to be part animal.

Tracey knew she should stop him, and she would. In just another minute. Tangling her tongue with Phoenix's beneath the light of an almost full moon with the August breeze wafting off the Atlantic to tease and tickle her senses was like the culmination of every fantasy she'd ever had.

Makes sense if you think about it. The man is inhumanly fast and strong. Growly, too.

Wonderful! She was starting to believe all the

crazy! Heck, was this even happening at all? Maybe she was still unconscious?

That made much more sense to her than thinking this gorgeous, giant, sexy hunk of hotness was actually devouring her mouth like she was air, and he needed her to survive. Things like that simply didn't happen to her. And yet. Here she was.

Tracey moaned as his hands traveled from her face down her shoulders to her waist, then hips. He didn't seem to mind the softness of her frame, the extra packaging on her ass and thighs as he squeezed and fondled her with exquisite care. Her panties were damp, and her breasts swelled with need under his careful ministrations.

Phoenix felt so good pressed up against her. Untamed and dangerous. His body was so big and warm. His stance was a heady combination of protective and possessive. She'd never felt so small and cherished as she did in his arms.

"Want you so bad," he growled, nipping her chin gently with his teeth and running his tongue along her jaw and neck.

Fuck me. That feels good.

"Mine," he growled, and the roughly whispered possessive verbiage sent spikes of desire shooting through her veins.

"Get a room!"

Phoenix broke the kiss, turning to growl at whoever yelled the embarrassing yet accurate suggestion. She pushed against him, and he stepped back, turning to face her immediately.

"Shit. I got carried away. Are you alright?" Phoenix asked.

Tracey nodded, but the truth was, no. She wasn't alright. Not in the least. Her heart was beating like a drum. She'd seen things that night that had her head spinning. The least of which was not the fact that two seconds ago she was practically having sex in public!

"Tracey, please look at me."

"So, you're saying you are like the Tiger I saw— what did you call yourself—*a Shifter?*"

"Yes. Shifters are dual natured, we live with our animals as part of ourselves," he explained.

"Well, are you even human at all? How does this work? Can I see your Wolf?" she asked, trying to reconcile the world she knew with the one Phoenix had introduced her to.

He took her hand, and she accepted his readily. No matter what was about to happen, Tracey had to be honest, if only to herself. She liked him. More than that. She felt right with him.

It was as if Tracey was more herself with him than with any other person at any other time in her entire life. How was that for a revelation?

"Yes, let me explain. I am a man, but I am more. Shifters share their souls with another creature that exists on a separate plane while we wear our human skin."

"So, Shifters are part animal?"

"Yes, and no. Our animals are not the same kind you see in the zoo or that live in the wild. They are imbued with magic. A spirit animal, but not so much totem as real and physically manifestable."

"So, this is real. You are real. What were you saying about mates?"

"Yes. I am real. And so are my feelings for you. Mates are what you would call soulmates. A mate is the one person who completes both sides of a Shifter. Other supes have mates too, but I can only tell you how it is for me."

"And you are a Wolf."

"Yes, sort of. My animal is a prehistoric species of Wolf. A Dire Wolf. My beast is ancient, and he is sure you are ours."

"Holy shit."

"Yes. I guess you could say that." Phoenix grinned and squeezed her hand. "There are a lot of different things out there, love. More than I could tell you about or that either of us could imagine—"

"Should I be scared?"

"Of me? Never."

"Why?"

"One thing at a time, love," his voice dropped as he spoke.

"Wait, did you say Dire Wolf? Like in that show?"

"Sort of," he replied. "Dire Wolves are prehistoric versions of the animals that roam so few and far between in the world today. Why are you grinning?"

"It's just, you're so tall and golden. Like your hair and skin. I would've thought you were an eagle or something." She shrugged.

"You thought I was a bird?"

He feigned insult, and Tracey couldn't hold in her laugh. Good. That felt good.

"I'm sorry, I didn't mean it as an insult."

"And you're my Dire Wolf, right?" she asked with a grin, and he looked thoughtful for a moment.

"Wait one second," he replied and looked around as if to ensure they were alone before he unzipped and divested himself of his jeans.

Tracey's mouth went dry. With his clothes on, Phoenix Tala was the most devastatingly handsome man she'd ever seen. Without them, he was a golden god.

A look of concern passed across his handsome face, but something made him hold his tongue. He stepped back, and Tracey held his gaze. Then, suddenly, the most incredible thing happened.

She watched with rapt attention as his whole body hummed and glowed with pulsating power. A shimmery sheen of golden light surrounded him. She heard the crack and rip of what must have been tendons and bones shattering and re-knitting themselves, but it was too quick for her to be sure. Then poof, Phoenix was gone, replaced by an enormous buff-colored animal.

Tracey gasped and covered her mouth with her hands. The creature was huge, bigger than any Wolf she'd ever seen at the zoo. Even larger than the special bred Great Danes her father kept when she was just a little girl. Of course, she was never allowed to play with those animals. Never allowed to pet them.

Her fingers itched as she stared at the well-behaved Wolf, who was her Phoenix. The beast sat on his haunches, unmoving, completely unthreatening. Under that warm, golden-aquamarine stare, her heart resumed its natural pace.

Tracey felt safe in his presence. Even more so, she felt protected, and something else. Some other elusive emotion emanated from the stunning creature.

"Phoenix?" she whispered his name softly, and the Wolf stood up.

Reaching out with one hand tentatively, she closed her eyes, afraid for a split second she'd misjudged and would soon be missing an appendage. But instead of sharp teeth, she felt soft fur beneath her fingertips.

Phoenix's Wolf padded towards her slowly. A soft whine escaped his massive maw, and Tracey giggled. She gasped when his cold nose nuzzled her palm, then moved up her arm, stopping at her wrist then on to her shoulder, neck, and cheek.

"Okay. You are much better than any old eagle," Tracey relented as she ran her hands over his beautiful coat.

He was so big and powerful. She felt the muscles of his chest, and the warmth of his skin beneath the thick, cream colored fur.

Beautiful beast. Dangerous. Sexy. Mine.

Suddenly, her hands were skimming flesh. The Wolf had retreated, and Phoenix was there once more, standing in the cradle of her thighs wearing nothing at all. His body emanated heat, but still she shivered.

Not because she was cold, but because, for the first time in her life, Tracey felt desired. His lusty gaze fell on her lips, and she tensed, ready for him to stake his claim.

"Come on, beautiful. Let's go before I lose my mind," he growled.

"But where are we going?" she asked as he tugged on his jeans.

"I promised you a ride. And I don't want to rush you, Tracey," he murmured, stealing a kiss before he shrugged his shirt on.

Tracey licked her lips. Yes, she wanted to go for a ride on his Harley, but that was not all she wanted. Was it? The question was, was she ready to do this? To run off with a Wolf biker and to hell with her old life.

Hell. Fucking. Yeah.

CHAPTER 16

"Are you okay?" Phoenix asked, his voice deep and husky.

"Uh huh," she replied, her voice a husky whisper in his ear.

"You sure?"

"Yes."

"Squeeze your legs tighter around my hips. Like that," he growled, unable to hide the Wolf.

"Okay," she whispered breathlessly in his ear.

"Is that alright?"

"Yes. It feels good."

"Good."

Next, Phoenix gunned the engine of the powerful machine between his legs. He and his Pack mates had added custom improvements to their bikes to support their massive weights, and the increased speeds they preferred. Not that he would speed with his mate riding behind him.

Her safety was tantamount to all else. His Wolf growled softly in his chest. The beast still preening that she'd approved of him. It had been touch and go for a moment back then. But she was brave, his mate. Strong and courageous.

Damn, she was sexy, calling to his beast with all the seductive force of a siren's song. Phoenix wanted nothing more than to sink into her wet heat, but he had other plans for wooing his mate first. And it started here and now, on his bike on a strip of sand behind the hotels and streets of Maccon City.

The docks and rocky shores of the intracoastal waterway were deserted at this time of night. Good thing. He was about to show his sweet Tracey how to ride.

"What if I fall off?"

She squeaked when he gunned the powerful engine and held his waist tighter. He did it again just to feel her squeeze him with her thighs. Okay, he was a jerk sometimes, but he never said he wasn't. This woman made him want things he'd never dreamed of.

He wanted her. All of her. The good, the bad, the

beautiful, and the gritty. She was so damned important, did she even know it? If not, it was his job to show her.

"I got you. I won't let anything bad happen to you, beautiful. Not while I live and breathe."

"You swear?"

"I swear. You trust me?"

"Yes. I know it's dumb, but I trust you more than anyone, Phoenix."

That single admission meant more to Phoenix than a thousand promises anyone else had or could have ever made to him. Tracey Donner was the best damn woman he'd ever seen, and he knew in his heart, his soul, and his beast, that she was the only one for him.

"Hold on to me, beautiful."

She did, and satisfaction rumbled through him. Phoenix loosed a short howl, then he took off. Speeding along the tightly packed rocky sand, Phoenix revved the engine and headed for the surf. Grinning madly while Tracey squealed with glee, the tires made the surf spray up to wet the two of them, but it was worth it.

Hearing her exuberance, the sheer joy flowing through her as they raced up and down the small strip, was worth the wet boots and jeans and a hell of a lot more. Happiness coursed through his veins, as he rolled to a stop a few feet from where they'd dropped his bedroll and backpack with some things he'd brought with him.

Marco had assured him this place would be empty, but he used his Shifter senses, anyway. Needed to make certain they were alone. His Wolf would tolerate no intrusions.

He wanted his mate. Needed her now. Alone.

Mine.

"That was incredible," Tracey said, still grinning.

Her lips were still red from the gloss she wore earlier or from biting them, he wasn't sure. So soft and sweet, like cherries and sin. He was dying for a taste.

The mood changed with the next breeze, and the earlier playfulness they shared receded. The moon was bright, an inch closer to full, and he could feel it pulling the tide and calling to his beast.

But he was not running tonight. Oh no. Tonight was not for fur. It was for skin. His and hers. Theirs.

"Phoenix," she whispered his name on a soft exhale, sending shivers down his spine.

He felt like a boy again. Young and green and desperate for a stolen kiss or a secret moment with his favorite girl. No doubt about it, Tracey made everything new and sweet, and so damn sexy.

Shit.

If he was not careful, this would be over before it began. He was trembling with need, dick pulsating in his pants, eager to burst. She was so damn potent. Her inner beauty called to him like nothing ever had.

Phoenix was falling more each second. Even now, the Dire Wolf demanded he claim her with his bite. He struggled with the creature, trying hard to rein in his beast. He needed to be gentle. To treat her tenderly. But fuck, was it hard.

"Uh uh," she whispered, pulling her mouth away from his. "I want all of you, Phoenix. Don't you dare hold back on me now."

"Mine," he growled, and claimed her mouth once more.

He was clumsy and unpracticed in his attempts to peel her clothes off, but she helped him. Unshy and surprisingly in control as she slid the tight dress down her hips and silky thighs.

Standing proud and bare breasted, with a sexy pair of hip hugging boy shorts on, Tracey appeared before him like a warrior goddess. His mouth went dry, cock straining in his wet jeans, and Phoenix's growl rose uncontrollably in his chest.

"You said I was your mate," she began.

"Yessss," he replied, voice thick with his Wolf.

"What does that mean?"

"I want to claim you with my bite. The Wolf needs to."

"Claim me?"

"Yes, I want you to be mine. My woman. My mate. My partner. Forever, sweet Tracey. There are no take backs for me if we do this. I will be bound to you for eternity."

"Forever might be long enough," she whispered, pulling those sexy little shorts off and revealing her entire beautiful self to him.

"Fuck, woman, you are killing me."

"Will it hurt?" she asked as she took a small step towards him.

"I'll take care of you first, beautiful."

"Alright then," she said, waiting, but he was frozen. Was this real? Did she really want to be his?

"Well? Are you going to claim me or not?"

"Fuck yessssss," Phoenix snarled.

His chest was heaving as she approached him slowly and carefully. Her face was all seriousness and gravity. Tracey stopped with only a hair's breadth between them.

"I want you to claim me, Phoenix. Tonight, I want to become yours, and I want you to be mine."

"Then I will, Tracey, tonight under the moon and stars, with the Fates blessing, I'm gonna make love to you. I'll give you my mating bite. It will tie us together in a bond no human or supernatural can ever break. We will be together, Tracey, you and I, a family, until the sun burns out in the sky or maybe even longer."

Phoenix stopped talking and waited. It was the hardest thing he ever had to do. Everything inside him said don't wait, claim her, kiss her, make love to her until she was screaming, begging for his bite. But she deserved so much more than that, and he refused to manipulate her. Finally, she lifted those creamy jade eyes to his.

"I want that too. No more waiting."

"No more waiting," he agreed.

Then she touched him, and the leash he had on his control broke with an audible snap.

Mine.

CHAPTER 17

Tracey was no virgin, but the way Phoenix was staring at her brought a rosy blush to her skin deeper than any other time she'd ever been naked in front of a man.

Maybe it was because he was so very handsome. Or maybe it was because they were technically in public, though this section seemed to be completely deserted.

Nah. It's because of him.

She felt the truth of that sentiment down to her toes. Phoenix loomed over her for a moment, tearing his clothes off in a whirl of movement that any other time would have made her head spin. But she was too caught up in the acres of tight, bronzed skin and the rippling muscles revealed to her.

Holy moly.

Her sexy Dire Wolf mate was incredible. And yes, he was hers. Had said so himself. She wasn't sure when she'd stopped believing in magic. Sometime when she was too young to have had such doubts.

Between fat camps and her parents' social engagements, Tracey had lost that naïve trust in all things fantastical every child should have. But she had it back now. In spades. He had done that.

Phoenix had restored her faith in magic. That same magic filled the very air she breathed. She felt it dance along her nerve endings, especially when she was kissing Phoenix.

Oh my.

The man sure could kiss. Her sex throbbed with need as he teased her senses with his expert caresses and multi-talented lips and tongue. Those torturously slow touches continued until she was mindless, aching, and desperate, all but begging him to give her what she needed. And all she needed was him.

"Good, mate. Want you to burn for me," he growled into her ear, sending her spiraling into ecstasy with the slightest of touches.

Mate. The word had sounded foreign to her ears when he'd first whispered it to her. Now she felt its rightness. It was like her mind, heart, body, and soul knew the meaning and wholeheartedly accepted it, accepted him.

Yes. She wanted him to claim her. To make her his in every way. Hell, she was impatient, flexing her hips in a silent plea for him to tend her where she wanted him most. But the big, frustrating, but oh-so-sexy man would not be rushed.

His mouth closed over one throbbing breast, teeth tugging on her tight nipple, and Tracey moaned aloud. Moisture dripped down her thighs, her sex readying itself for his invasion. She could feel the hot, hard, and heavy press of his magnificently thick and long cock on her thigh.

Fuck. So good.

She could hardly wait to have him deep inside her. Knew without a doubt he would not leave her wanting. Phoenix would take care of her needs. Every single one of them.

Still, he was being damned obstinate about it. She panted as he moved to her other breast, sucking her nipple while his blunt fingers edged closer and closer to her aching pussy. Phoenix seemed satisfied to take his time, but Tracey was dying.

"Please," she whimpered as one thick digit traced

her nether lips, only to pull away before he really touched her.

Her hands wound in his thick, blond locks, and she tried pushing him down her body, but he was immovable. Looking down, she was a smile teasing the corner of his lips.

Oh, so that's how it's gonna be.

Tracey growled a little like a Wolf herself, then pushed his shoulders, making him lift up so that she could reach between them. Once she held her prize, his eyes flashed to hers. The golden-aquamarine gaze of his beast glittered as she pumped his iron-hard shaft with her fist, tracing the pearl of precum that dripped from his slit.

"Tracey," he grunted.

"What?"

"Fuck, baby, you gotta stop that."

"Why?"

"Because I won't last a minute. Need you."

"Good. Then take me already, Wolf. Make me yours," she commanded.

With a deep, guttural growl, Phoenix pulled his hips out of her reach and slid down her body, draping her legs over his shoulders. Her sex quivered in anticipation. She'd never been good at this, but with Phoenix, she felt like a fucking goddess.

"Need to taste you," he grunted and without pause, closed his hot, wet mouth over her pussy in a searing kiss that tore a scream from her throat.

"Fuck, beautiful, you're delicious," he growled and drove his tongue into her again.

Licking her from her clit to her asshole and back again, Phoenix left no inch of her unexplored. A primal growl seemed to rise from his chest as he continued to devour her slick flesh.

She was completely undone. Her body wound tight, she grabbed his hair, holding on for dear life. Her man was pure magic, and he was eating her like she was ambrosia. Heat pulsed through her, and she felt the stirrings of something amazing about to happen.

Close. So close.

Finally, he pushed her over the edge, and Tracey came, gushing like an uncontrollable tide. Fierce, hot pleasure shot through her body, wave after wave of inexpressible feeling as her body flew into bliss. She was conscious of him, his beautiful mouth still lapping at her heat, but she was too raw to come down yet. She still needed.

As if he knew it—*like he could read her mind*—Phoenix reared up. His masculine growl filled the air as he spread her legs wide, baring her for his steady stare, his eyes filled with need and possession.

"S'beautiful, mate. Gonna make you come for me again. Want that? Want me to make this pussy mine?"

"Yes. Oh yes," she pleaded.

Phoenix palmed his thick cock, placing the mushroomed tip at her slick entrance. His long fingers grabbed her hips, and his gaze never left hers as he pushed himself inside.

One. Inch. At. A. Time.

And he did slowly—*so damned slow*—Tracey thought she would die before he filled her. Finally, his hips were flush against hers, and he stayed there for a beat, maybe two. Then the bastard withdrew.

"No!" She screamed, scratching at his shoulders.

"Easy, mate. I got what you need," he growled and lowered his hips again.

Over and over he drove into her, each time his cock stroked her inner walls just right, taking her to the brink of pleasure, but pulling out before she hit that pinnacle.

Fucking Wolf was a beast. Her tits bounced as he pumped harder, faster, and she envied him his teeth and claws. She wanted to claim him, to mark him sure as she wanted him to bite her flesh and declare her his to the whole damned world.

She'd never felt this wild drive to be possessed, but she wanted it now. Needed it.

"Phoenix," she moaned his name.

The fucker laughed. The deep, masculine sound was thick with his Wolf. He knew exactly what he was doing to her, and she was already plotting her revenge. Tracey was sure she could treat him to the same delicious torment.

Oh, the pleasure she would get in circling his broad-headed cock with her tongue. Licking the drop of precum she knew would seep from his slit. She would fondle his heavy balls, tease the sensitive skin there, while she lapped along the rim with the flat of her tongue.

Oh yeah.

She could do that. She would do that. Right after he made her come again.

"So hot. So sexy. Mine," he growled, and doubled his efforts.

Thrust, flex, withdraw, and repeat.

Fuck, Tracey couldn't think anymore. Both she and Phoenix were writhing against each other. His invasion deeper, heavier, faster, and harder as he pounded into her so damn good.

"So tight, love. You're squeezing me so good," he growled.

She wanted to speak, to say something about the magnificent stretching *oh so good burn* his cock was treating her to, but she was incapable at the moment. She needed more of that delicious friction, wanted more of him. Deeper, faster, harder. And just like that, he was moving again. No more playing. Phoenix's palms held her down gently by her wide hips and she retaliated by wrapping her legs tight around his waist.

In an out, in a dance old as time, he pumped, and she swiveled. Together, they moved in time until Tracey could hardly breathe. Just when she thought she couldn't go any higher, he pushed her to another level. She tasted the salt on his skin as she kissed everywhere she could reach.

Their moans and the sounds of skin slapping against skin filled her ears, drowning out even the ocean. And why shouldn't it? This was bigger, deeper, and more eternal than any sea.

Phoenix Tala was laying claim to her, and she, Tracey Donner, would be alone no more.

"Tracey," he growled, pumping his hips harder and deeper.

"Tracey."

He called her name again.

"Tracey!"

Once more and she was spiraling.

"Tracey. Mate," he snarled.

This time his mouth, full of fangs, flashed in her peripheral vision and her core heated, tightening around him, until she thought she'd burst into flames. Then, pain exploded in her shoulder, interrupting the burning pleasure pulsing in her very blood. The hurt lasted only a moment before her pleasure increased tenfold.

"Phoenix!" Tracey screamed his name, scratching at his shoulders.

Red hot flames consumed her, and she thought she saw them encircling their bodies, Phoenix's shocked gaze met hers as he released her flesh, roaring loudly as his movements turned jerky. She felt the force of his orgasm slamming into her. Warm hot jets of his cum filled her, sending another climax spurring through Tracey's body.

Eons later...or maybe just minutes...

Her body hummed with pleasure. Her heart was swollen with emotion. Shock at the beauty of the lights that still floated in the air, some kind of magical afterglow from their mating.

"Mate," Tracey sighed the word as she snuggled into the warm embrace of her mate and lover.

"You're magic, beautiful," he whispered.

Phoenix's big body curled around hers on the blanket he'd laid out for them, protecting them from the coarse sand. After he'd emptied himself inside of her, he'd pulled her on him, till she was practically using him as a mattress. A position she had no quarrel with.

Maybe a lifetime ago it would have bothered her, but she felt no shame or embarrassment. Tracey was all curves and thickness, but her mate seemed to love it. He could not stop touching her.

Now that he'd claimed her, she wondered if his desire would lessen. But she knew in an instant, their passion would only grow. It was like Tracey could see and hear inside his very heart.

"It's the matebond," he whispered, kissing her head and cupping her ass with his hand.

"Can we read each other's minds?" she wondered aloud.

"Not really, but maybe in time. It's more like we can feel each other's emotions."

Tracey breathed deep, and as incredible as it seemed, she dug within herself, amazed at the pulsing bond she felt between them.

"You love me," she said aloud in shock at the force of feeling that flowed into her from him.

"I love you," he replied, and she felt joy emanating from his admission.

Holy cow. Phoenix Tala loved her. He would protect her, would be her safe haven. And even more amazing, he liked her, too. She grinned and kissed his chest as happiness seemed to flow from him to her. It was unlike anything she'd ever felt. So pure and light, warm too.

Like magic. Like fate.

"It is fate. You are my destiny, Tracey, and I am yours."

The rightness of that sentiment poured through her along with all the feeling and thoughts he had in his mind. It was like a river of information, and Tracey wept at the beauty of it. She knew his heart, and it was time she trusted hers as well.

"I love you too," she confessed, leaning up to kiss his lips.

"Good. Come here," he growled and pressed his mouth to hers.

Heat pooled between her legs and Tracey moaned as he cupped her sex with his callused fingers.

"My turn," he growled.

CHAPTER 18

Phoenix's Dire Wolf growled contentedly once he had his woman back at the hotel, inside his bed. They'd dressed quickly when the rain had started, laughing as they went. He did not know what to make of the blast of gold fire that had encapsulated them when he claimed her, but fuck, it was amazing.

She was amazing. His beast insisted he get her warm and safe after their outdoor romps, and he had, first with a shower, then inside his bed. He was insatiable for the woman, and if she'd ever harbored any doubt about his attraction to her, Phoenix had laid that all to rest over the past few hours.

She stirred beside him, and his cock stood to

attention again. Sexy woman did not know what she did to him with her little moans and groans. Her tanned skin glowed in the darkness of the room, and her delicious feminine scent, like sugar cookies and something else, was now mingled with the fur and spice of his Wolf.

He looked at the bite he'd given her on her shoulder, frowning at the hurt it had caused, even if only momentarily. Amazingly enough, she seemed to heal fast, which was astounding since he didn't think humans could heal that quickly.

Phoenix had sent a text to Derrick, explaining to his Alpha that he'd found his mate, and the man congratulated him. He could not wait for her to meet his Pack, but first, he wanted to take her on a trip. She'd planted the notion in his brain before they'd fallen asleep last night. And it was thoughts of ways to fulfill her desires that had woken him up.

"Will you take me to see the world, Phoenix? Just you and me and your bike?"

"Anything, my love. I would do anything for you."

And he would. That much was true. He'd already started planning, but first, they had to make one stop. She might not like it, but Phoenix believed in closure, and his sweet mate deserved some.

"Your thoughts are too loud," Tracey moaned, pressing her curvaceous backside against his cock as he spooned her from behind.

Phoenix hissed. Fuck, she was gorgeous.

"Mmm, you feel good, woman."

"Mmm, good. I want you to make me feel good, mate," she said, and fuck if he was not ready for the challenge.

Phoenix cupped her soft tits, squeezing them as he rocked his hips, sliding his cock between her slick folds. He kissed and nipped her neck and shoulders, loving the feel of her ripe ass cushioning his hips. He was a rutting beast for the woman. She called to his primal side, and there was nothing he would not do for her.

"Lift your ass up, beautiful. Like that," he growled, turning to kneel behind her as she lay down on her belly.

Tracey lifted her ass, spreading her legs for him and fuck, she was gorgeous. Her sex glistened, dripping with her arousal as he traced her crack with his thick fingertips, all the way till he reached her swollen nubbin.

"Need you," she moaned, pressing back and rubbing against his dick.

"Gonna make you crazy first," he growled.

Phoenix was so damned hot for her. He leaned forward and plunged his tongue into her heated core, rubbing her clit with one hand, while he teased her forbidden hole with his other.

He felt her pussy quiver and tremble, and before she finished shouting his name, he covered her. Pushing deep inside her slick pussy as her orgasm started had Phoenix crossing his eyes with how good she felt.

Nothing else existed while he was buried in her sweet body. There were only the two of them. Tracey was everything good and beautiful and pure in this world, and he would do awful things to keep her safe, cherished, protected, and by his side.

"Love you, mate," he growled as ecstasy took hold.

He gritted his teeth, determined to keep her right there with him. But he didn't have to wait long. Her body was responsive, reacting to his as if she were made for him—and she was, he supposed.

"Phoenix!" she yelled his name, her walls tightening around him.

Her next release rocketed through to him, and fuck, he had no choice now. Hot jets of cum pulsed from his cock, filling her as he bucked into her mindlessly. He moved until he was empty, completely, and totally undone by what they had shared.

"You are part of me now, Tracey. The best part," he grunted, withdrawing so he could clean her and care for her.

Sweet, strong woman. My woman.

T*wo days later...*

Phoenix cleared his throat as he sat in the clinical greeting room in the Donner's home. He would've rather been sitting anywhere else in the world. Tracey had not been happy about this little detour, but he was determined she should get some closure for all her pain.

From what his mate had told him of her family, his justifiable anger on her behalf for the way she'd been treated by those who should've loved her most was not out of place. He understood her reasons for not wanting to visit the cold estate where she'd grown up.

But Tracey should have some of her own things before they embarked on their life together. She should be able to look the people she came from in the eye and let them know they did not break her. No other woman he'd ever known was as deserving of respect and love as this woman.

He would give her that. He would give her everything.

She'd tried calling her parents when they'd arrived at the posh manor, and she was waiting for them to video conference her back from the yacht where they were spending the rest of the season.

Meanwhile, she had some of her things to collect, and as for the rest, she had planned to have everything packed up and sent to the Pack house behind *Serious Moonlight*.

"Phoenix, this is Rosa."

His mate's face beamed as she returned to the sitting room with an older female in tow. The woman looked kind and genuinely happy to see Tracey if the fierce hug she gave her was any indication.

"Hello, Rosa. I'm Phoenix."

"Oh, my Tracey! He is a handsome one. Nice to meet you," she said, then turned back to his mate with unshed tears in her eyes.

"I am so glad to see you. Look at you! So carefree and happy. You look beautiful, *linda*," the woman cried.

Phoenix smiled, pleased to see someone who'd cared for his sweet mate while she'd been growing up in that cold and hostile home. Rosa released Tracey and his mate rushed to him. Her emotions were high, and her jade eyes sparkled with unshed tears.

"It is nice to meet you," he told the other woman and took her offered hand, bending down to kiss her cheek.

She had the same sugar cookie scent about her as Tracey and he paused a moment, wondering why that was.

"I see you," the woman whispered into his ear, a grin teasing the corner of her mouth.

Before he could question the odd statement, the laptop Tracey had set up on the coffee table beeped and soon Tracey's parents were there.

"Hello? Tracey? What is this about, young lady?"

Daniel Donner frowned into the camera, giving himself a double chin. Clearly, he was not a technology fan.

"Well, what is it? I see you came back with your

tail between your legs after embarrassing us like that. Ha. See, I told you," Daniella Donner snapped.

She turned her heavily made-up face to her husband with a waspish expression that boiled Phoenix's blood. The couple looked nothing like his beautiful mate, and again, he could not reconcile their familial connection. Lucky for him, she was different from these cold, unfeeling people.

"See. She is back. Just like I knew she would be, Daniel."

"Wow," Tracey replied. "I was gone for days and that's how you talk to me. You don't even ask me how I am?" Tracey questioned, and his Dire Wolf growled.

She squeezed his hand, stilling his urge to close the laptop and disconnect from those two scowling faces.

"What is it you want, Tracey?" her father barked the question.

"Hi, Dad. Nice to see you, too," Tracey said to her father. "You know, Mom, I used to want to be like you when I was a child. Beautiful and poised, but now I know nothing I ever do will earn your favor."

"You could never be like me," his mate's mother returned nastily.

"Tracey, what your mother means is you simply don't have the constitution. Now, I suggest you come home and forget this whole mess—"

Phoenix could not believe his ears. These people were the worst. How horrible did someone have to be to treat their own child this way? His Wolf was pissed, but the beast understood she needed his support, not his anger. The animal stilled inside of him, waiting in case she needed him.

"Sir, Ma'am, I think you should both just quiet down and listen to your daughter—"

"Wait a second, who is that?" her mother screeched.

"Tracey! What is that strange man doing in my house?" her father demanded.

"Mom, Dad, this is Phoenix. He is with me," Tracey replied, and straightened her shoulders.

Phoenix moved to her side, offering her his strength and support lovingly and freely. He probably should have worn something other than worn denim and his leather cut, but they'd ridden up on his bike, and Phoenix believed in comfort above all. He'd even gotten her a pair of sexy as fuck jeans and a black leather vest fitted over a ripped up t-shirt with the *Serious Moonlight* logo on it.

"Mr. And Mrs. Donner," he growled, unable to keep the hostility out of his voice.

"Oh my God! Tracey! What are you wearing? You ran off with a biker?! This is just more embarrassment!" His mate's mother screeched.

"What does it matter if he rides a motorcycle, Mother? He makes me happy. I make him happy. And I didn't come back with my tail between my legs, I came back to tell you I am leaving home for good. I am going to be with Phoenix, and we are going to see the world," she told her parents, turning her head to flash him that thousand watt grin he loved.

His whole body responded to her happiness, vibrating with pride and need. He wanted to kiss her, hold her, tell her how brave she was to face these two horrible, uncaring people. It was obvious they were not the tender, doting parents she deserved, and the loss was theirs. Tracey was fucking wonderful. He would tell her that, too. As soon as they left this house, that felt colder than a cemetery to him and his beast.

"I forbid it," Daniel Donner yelled, wagging his pasty finger on the screen.

"The hell you do," Phoenix growled, the threat of

someone forbidding his mate anything had the animal riled.

"You see how she really is? I told you, Daniel," Tracey's mother yelled, a look of poisonous triumph on her face.

"How can you ruin us this way?" her father asked.

"Dad, this is not about you. Try to understand."

"After everything I did for you. I tried to raise her correctly, Daniel, but look at the girl. She could never be the daughter we deserved," her waspish mother griped.

Phoenix could barely contain his growl. Tracey tried to reason, but her parents' vicious insults and demands would not be silenced. At least, not until Rosa stepped in.

"Enough!" Rosa said in a loud, clear voice that emanated with power.

"You will both stop this right now. Years I have watched you fail to rise to the honor of being her parents."

"Rosa, I don't think—" Tracey's father replied, but his sentence was cut off by Rosa's sharp hiss.

Good for Rosa.

Phoenix growled, in full agreement with the slight woman.

"Tell her the truth now."

Phoenix's jaw dropped as the older woman's façade faded away. No longer was she the Donner's housekeeper. Rosa was something else. Something that smelled distinctly like sugar cookies and Tracey. Her age lines receded, gray hair turned black, and those muddy brown eyes lightened to a creamy jade —much like his mate's.

"Rosa?" Tracey gasped, covering her mouth with both hands. Phoenix moved behind her, placing his large hands lightly on her shoulders.

"*Oh linda*, I am still your Rosa. Daniel and Daniella Donner, you were charged with raising this daughter of the *Doñas de fuera* until she could find her way. We had assumed you would treat her with love and dignity, but you have failed in this. Now, you owe her the truth," she announced.

"Rosa? What are you talking about?" Tracey asked, a hiccup in her voice told him how emotional she was feeling.

"Finally!" Daniella Donner screeched again. "I am not your mother. I never was. Your father here cheated on me! And you, you were the fruit of his misguided affair. To think I had to take you into my home and raise you. My husband's bastard! I never even wanted kids."

"What are you saying?" Tracey asked. She gasped

again as tears fell from her eyes, and Phoenix squeezed her to him tightly.

"Tracey, it is true," Daniel said, and the insect cleared his throat. "I was young and foolish, and Thea was very beautiful—"

"Oh, please," Daniella hissed.

"Shut up, Daniella. Thea was beautiful and Rosa is right, we did a lousy job raising my daughter. Tracey, I am sorry if we failed you," the man said, and to Phoenix's preternatural hearing, he truly sounded remorseful.

"Tracey, there are things you need to know," Rosa said, turning to face his shivering mate.

"I can't," she said, shaking her head.

Phoenix wanted to pick her up and run out of there, but he knew something incredible was about to reveal itself. Tracey deserved to know her truth, and he would be right beside her to give support and anything else she might need.

"Hey, you got this, beautiful. I am staying right here with you, and I won't let anything harm you, I promise," he vowed.

"Okay. If you're with me, I can do this," she said, and her gaze flicked back to Rosa.

"You have found a good mate, Tracey," Rosa said

approvingly. "Now, to begin, I suppose I should tell you that your father, Daniel, met my grandniece on a business trip. They had an affair, and she became pregnant. We of the *Doñas de fuera* have mixed our bloodlines with humans for thousands of years."

"But what does that mean?"

"Ah, I see. Well, the *Doñas de fuera* literal translation is *women of the outside*."

"Outside?" Tracey asked.

"Witches," Phoenix replied. he had heard tales of mysterious women but thought they had been driven from this world by that mad machine that was the Inquisition.

"I see your mate knows our history. And true, Torquemada's reign had almost destroyed us with the Inquisition, but we are a resistant breed. Not just Witch, *linda*. The *Doñas de fuera* have Fae blood," Rosa enlightened them.

"I'm a fairy?" Tracey blurted, and gods, he could not have loved her more.

"*Mmmm*, sort of. Your mother was just a quarter, making you a little less, but my dear, we are people of the arts. Your love of sewing and your creativity are blessings. I came to live with you to ensure you were being nurtured and treated well, just in case you developed powers of your own. I did all I could without directly interfering."

"Is that why you were always watching and waiting with cookies and tea? You were protecting me. Heck, you were always more mother to me than she ever was, Rosa."

"I tried my best to stay out of the most of it. This is not a kind world, *linda*, but you are a shining light amongst all the gloom. Your powers will be coming in faster now that you have met your mate. His Wolf will call to that wild side of you. Embrace it, my love. You will be better for it, I swear. I am so grateful I was here to see you find your feet. Your mother would have been proud—"

"What happened to her?"

"She passed away the night you were born. I am so sorry. I have a picture for you though, here," Rose said and removed a chain with a heart locket hanging from it from around her neck.

She handed it to Tracey, inside was the image of a woman with long blonde hair and the same green eyes staring back at her. On the other side of the image was a picture of a baby. It was Tracey.

"It is yours now," Rosa said.

Tracey gasped and handed the chain and locket

to Phoenix, who fastened it around her neck while she bravely tried to stop crying.

"I always felt so out of place here. Now I know why," she whispered. "But I was so happy with you, Rosa."

"I have loved every minute I got to spend on this plane with you, but I have to return home to our realm. Like many Fae, the *Doñas de fuera* have retreated from this plane. But should you ever need me, just think of me and I will get the message," Rosa told her before hugging Tracey, then Phoenix.

"I am so proud of you, my Tracey. You and your mighty Dire Wolf mate will be blessed, I have fore-seen it. He will be your champion now."

"I will. I swear it. I would do anything for her, Rosa. You have my word," Phoenix pledged.

"I know, Wolf. Like I said, I see you," she told him.

"Tracey?" her father called her name from the laptop, and his mate turned to face him after Rosa winked out of their plane of existence.

"I am not ready to discuss this with you. Not yet, and maybe not ever."

"I understand. All I can say is I am sorry," her father replied.

"I've left an address for my things to be forwarded. Rosa put it all in boxes already and a delivery company will be by in a few days. Goodbye."

Phoenix growled deep in his throat, closing the laptop before Tracey's stepmother's cruel words could reach his mate's ears. She was other, true, but her magic seemed to be tied to her love of art, and her innate beauty.

He couldn't wait to travel the path to finding out more about her supernatural nature at her side. His sweet Tracey. Beautiful mate. So full of surprises.

"You ready?" he asked.

"As I will ever be," she told him, closing the door on her past, ready to live in the now.

They left soon after, and he heaved a sigh of relief as Tracey snuggled up behind him on the massive Harley. He felt her wonder and curiosity, smiling to himself because he knew she would be fine. They had each other now.

"I love you. You know that, right?"

"You better," she returned and nipped his back with her blunt teeth.

"I do, mate. And I will prove it every damn day I get to live on this planet with you," he growled, and she beamed at him.

"I love you, too."

They sped off, eating up the miles, both their hearts beating in unison. Phoenix didn't think anything in the world could top the high of riding his Screamin' Eagle with his gorgeous mate clinging to his back.

It was pure fucking heaven.

EPILOGUE

Serious *Moonlight* was busy despite it being a Wednesday. He bypassed the roadhouse and parked his bike just outside the Pack House.

His Pack mates already knew they were coming, after a few days on the road, sightseeing, he wanted Tracey to meet everyone and have some downtime before he took her to visit South America, like she wanted. Gods, he loved that woman. Like nothing else in this world. She was everything to him.

He held open the door for her, greeted by a chorus of shouts as his Pack came forward one at a time. She squeaked when Derrick grabbed her for a hug, followed by a very pregnant Lucy.

"I am so happy to meet you," the Alpha fem said, lip trembling. She was so emotional these days.

"Thank you. I'm happy to meet you, too."

And so on, she went down the line, taking the claps to her shoulders, and quick hugs like a champ. Dire Wolves were touchy feely things, after all.

Tracey's hand gripped his, and he smiled down at his beautiful mate's pretty little head while she watched curiously as one of their biggest members lifted the sacred chest with his magicked ink and bamboo quills from their special spot on the shelf.

"Thor is favored by the gods. The old graybeard in our first MC called him that," Weylin explained.

"What does it mean?" she whispered.

"Well," Lucy interrupted, rubbing her protruding belly. "It means he's gonna close his eyes and get a vision of your future with this ol' puppy doggy right here, then he's gonna ink it on his back."

"Really?" Thor muttered from across the room. But the big man wasn't annoyed. Not really.

"A tattoo?" Tracey gasped.

"Yep. Don't worry. He does fine work," Sheila, the only female Dire Wolf in the Pack, inserted.

"'Sup, Phoenix?" Leo, her Lion mate, asked.

"Good to see you, bro. Tracey, that's Leo, he's Sheila's mate and a cop."

"You're a Dire Wolf, too?" she asked.

"What? No way. I am a far superior species of Shifter," he told her with a wink. "I am a Lion. Ooof!"

Sheila elbowed him right in the gut, rolling her eyes at the man.

"Superior, my ass," she muttered.

"I was just kidding," he wheezed, and Tracey snorted a laugh.

"OMG! She snorts. How fucking cute are you?" Lucy gushed, hugging her again.

"Okay, um, there, there," Tracey replied, uncertainty in her voice.

"I got this," Derrick said, and lifted his mate up, snuggling her on the couch to Phoenix's, and his mate's, relief.

Phoenix looked around at the lot of them, his Pack. There were four mated pairs with him and Tracey now. The rest were still searching. And with any luck, they would find their Fate soon enough.

Phoenix felt the ties that bound them warm and tighten. Yes, he was going to take Tracey on a road trip, but they would be back. After all, this was their Pack.

"This is home," Tracey whispered, looking up at him with stars in her creamy jade depths.

She understood his heart's desires even before he voiced them, and though he understood it was fast, too fast for *normals* but not for his mate who was something *other*—he loved her so much it hurt. A good kind of hurt. The kind that told him he was alive and one lucky sonofabitch.

"Kneel."

Thor's voice had that deep, monosyllabic tone that told everyone there he was in the middle of his vision. Phoenix's pulse raced. This was a defining moment in his history. An event he'd envisioned for a very long time.

Dire Wolves' lifespans were longer than normal Shifters, and as such, his mate's would increase and match his, drawing on their bond to give her longevity.

"Tonight, I gift you with your claiming tattoo. Wear it proudly, my Dire Wolf brother," Thor growled, eyes glowing in the dimly lit room.

Silence fell across the crowd. Phoenix heard nothing except the sound of Tracey's heartbeat and the soft flow of her tears as he turned away from Thor. His mate watched as the male etched their future into Phoenix's back.

Sheila, Ariella, and Lucy bracketed her on either side, the three had become quick friends, and he hoped Tracey would form a bond with them, as well.

She was good like that. Open and kind, she deserved to have real friends, sisters of the heart.

How could they resist her? He certainly hadn't been able to. His mate was so brave, watching each slice Thor made across his skin.

"There's so much blood," she whispered.

"He isn't hurting him, sweetie," Sheila whispered.

"He's a tough old dog," Lucy seconded.

Phoenix found her with his eyes, and her tears stilled. So much courage and pride shone on her face. She straightened her back, offering him bravery in the face of one of their most sacred rituals.

The bamboo quills cut deep, deeper than any other tattoo needle would have during a typical inking. It had to be that way to really scar the skin, otherwise his supernatural abilities would heal him far too quickly. Combined with the magicked ink, the tattoo would last as long as he and their love did.

Eternity.

His Dire Wolf howled inside of him. The ceremony was rigorous and long. Hours later, Thor dropped the last quill onto the floor, next to the other dozen he'd used, and slumped over on his side. Derrick kneeled down, offering Phoenix a hand while Leo and Brock lifted the Enforcer and brought him to his room to recover.

"Congrats, bro," the Pack Alpha said.

"Thank you, Alpha. What is it?" Phoenix's eyes flashed to Tracey's, unable to wait.

His mate had stayed the entire time, waiting patiently while his claiming tattoo was etched onto his skin. He had others, of course, but they were small compared to the massive piece Thor had just given him, guided by the gods themselves.

Phoenix was aware of Tracey walking behind him. Derrick had already moved away, giving them space. The Alpha helped Lucy sit down on the couch. Phoenix had a moment of concern for Thor, but he knew he was in good hands. The Wolf was always exhausted after channeling the gods during one of these rituals. He sucked in a breath, waiting for Tracey's reaction as he felt her slide to her knees.

"Oh, Phoenix," she whispered, and the tremble in her voice rocked him to his soul.

"What? What is it, love?"

"It's beautiful."

The others moved to see the image too, but he didn't care what they thought. Only Tracey's feelings mattered.

As it should be, his Wolf pushed the thought at him, and he accepted it.

The beast was right. Her emotions were the only ones that meant anything to him.

"Tell me."

"It's your Wolf, baying at the full moon and a woman—"

"Not a woman, you," he corrected.

"Yes," she said, and he heard the smile in her voice. "*Me.* I'm standing beside you, a baby in my arms. We're shrouded in gold lights. There are spirals that look like roads on a map, a cross, a needle, the moon, the sun, and waves. It's like a roadmap of our life together. Ruins in the background, a skyscraper on the left, a field of daisies in the distance—but I've never seen these things or places before."

Phoenix turned and pulled her to him. His heart was so full, it damn near burst. Gods, he loved her so much. She was so beautiful, heart, mind, body, and soul.

"We'll go together, mate. We will see the world beside one another. We will make a family. We will be each other's home."

"And when you're done, y'all will come back here where you belong. You're Pack now, Tracey Donner," Lucy butted in, and Phoenix felt his mate's happiness surging through him as if it was his own.

"Enough, mate. Let's leave these two alone," Derrick growled and picked his woman up and out of the room.

"Maybe she doesn't want to be alone with him," Lucy answered her husband.

"Yeah, I do. Every night from now until the day I die," Tracey whispered as she tilted her head for a kiss.

"Forever," Phoenix growled, claiming her lips with all the love he had for her in his soul.

He'd left the Pack House less than a week ago, and he was back now with his mate in tow, even if only for a little while. But they would be back. Roaming was fun for a little while, but this was where they would grow their roots.

"Forever sounds good, but what is time anyway, when you have your mate?" Tracey asked, grinning. She'd learned fast that they could communicate through their *matebond*. That little gift was not true telepathy, but they could send feelings and emotions, sometimes messages too, all without opening their mouths.

"Some might experience forever in a night."

"Is that so? Wanna test that theory?" he asked, kissing her sweet mouth.

"Hell yeah," she asserted. "I felt that way with you

that first hot night we met. Like I'd known you forever, Phoenix Tala."

"Me too, mate. Me too."

"I love you."

Phoenix exhaled, his entire body trembling with joy, need, and gratitude. He was one lucky Dire Wolf.

To have found his kick ass fated mate and to have earned her love was the greatest accomplishment of his life. He would cherish her.

Always.

"I love you too, Tracey Donner."

Then he lifted her up, carrying her to his old bedroom, and he showed her.

Again and again.

Bodies surging together, entwined in that ancient communion of flesh and souls, Phoenix and Tracey loved each other till the sun came up. They climbed higher with each coming together, exploding into the pure ecstatic bliss only true fated couples ever experienced. He was whole for the first time in his life. And she, well, she was everything to him.

After breakfast, they got on his bike and headed for the border. He'd promised to show her the world, and he was going to start right now. He was in no rush, after all, they had the rest of their lives.

"You ready, love?"

"I'm ready, mate."

Love really was an adventure, and theirs was just beginning.

T*he end.*

Liked this story? Want more Dire Wolf Mates?
Grab the next book, Love That Sass, at https://www.
cdgorri.com.book/love-that-sass.
Or
Follow the whole series at https://www.cdgorri.com/seres/
dire-wolf-mates.

Thank you and happy reading!

BEWARE... HERE BE DRAGONS!

The Falk Clan Tales began as my stories surrounding four dragon Brothers and how they find their one true mates, but when a long lost brother arrives on the scene, followed by a few more Shifters…what can I say? The more the merrier!

Each Dragon's chest is marked with his rose, the magical link to his heart and his magic. They each have a matching gemstone to go with it.

She's given up on love. But he's just begun.

In The Dragon's Valentine we meet the eldest Falk brother, Callius. He is on a mission to find a Castle and his one true mate, one he can trust with his diamond rose....

His heart is frozen. Can she change his mind about love?

In The Dragon's Christmas Gift our attention shifts to Alexsander, the youngest brother of the four. He has resigned himself to a life alone, until he meets *her*.

Some wounds run deep. Can a Dragon's heart be unbroken?

The Dragon's Heart is the story of Edric Falk who has vowed never to love again, but that changes when he meets his feisty mate, Joselyn Curacao.

She just wants a little fun. He's looking for a lifetime.

We finally meet Nikolai Falk and his sexy Shifter mate in The Dragon's Secret.

She doesn't believe in fairytales, until a Dragon comes knocking on her door.

Meet Castor Falk, the long lost brother of our original four Dragons, and his sassy mate Josette. The Dragon's Treasure is full of adventure and laughs.

Nothing can surprise this six hundred-year-old Dragon, except maybe her.

Devine Graystone meets his match in Sunny Daye, an irrepressible Wolf Shifter with a heart of gold. Read their story in The Dragon's Surprise.

He's a hardcore realist until she dares him to dream.

Nicholas Gravestone doesn't know what to think when he spies Minerva Lykos on the property his Dragon covets. Can this unlikely pair come to a truce? Find out in The Dragon's Dream.

Thanks for reading.

xoxo,

C.D.

*Dragon Mates & Dragon Mates 2 boxed sets are now available in hardcover, paperback, and ebook.

HAVE YOU MET MY BEARS?

Looking for a Paranormal Romance series that is loads of growly fun?

Meet the Barvale Clan first in the Bear Claw Tales! A complete shifter romance series about 4 brothers who discover and need to win their fated mates!

Followed by two more spin off series, the Barvale Clan Tales and the Barvale Holiday Tales!

No cliffhangers. Steamy PNR fun.
Go and read your next happily ever after today!

OTHER TITLES BY C.D. GORRI

Other Titles by C.D. Gorri

Paranormal Romance Books:

Macconwood Pack Novel Series:

Charley's Christmas Wolf: A Macconwood Pack Novel 1

Cat's Howl: A Macconwood Pack Novel 2

Code Wolf: A Macconwood Pack Novel 3

The Witch and The Werewolf: A Macconwood Pack Novel 4

To Claim a Wolf: A Macconwood Pack Novel 5

Conall's Mate: A Macconwood Pack Novel 6

Her Solstice Wolf: A Macconwood Pack Novel 7

Werewolf Fever: A Macconwood Pack Novel 8

Also available in 2 boxed sets:

The Macconwood Pack Volume 1

The Macconwood Pack Volume 2

Macconwood Pack Tales Series:

Wolf Bride: The Story of Ailis and Eoghan A

Macconwood Pack Tale 1

Summer Bite: A Macconwood Pack Tale 2

His Winter Mate: A Macconwood Pack Tale 3

Snow Angel: A Macconwood Pack Tale 4

Charley's Baby Surprise: A Macconwood Pack Tale 5

Home for the Howlidays: A Macconwood Pack Tale 6

A Silver Wedding: A Macconwood Pack Tale 7

Mine Furever: A Macconwood Pack Tale 8

A Furry Little Christmas: A Macconwood Pack Tale 9

Also available in two boxed sets:

The Macconwood Pack Tales Volume 1

Shifters Furever: The Macconwood Pack Tales Volume 2

<u>The Falk Clan Tales:</u>

The Dragon's Valentine: A Falk Clan Novel 1

The Dragon's Christmas Gift: A Falk Clan Novel 2

The Dragon's Heart: A Falk Clan Novel 3

The Dragon's Secret: A Falk Clan Novel 4

The Dragon's Treasure: A Falk Clan Novel 5

The Dragon's Surprise: A Falk Clan Novel 6

The Dragon's Dream: A Falk Clan Novel 7

Dragon Mates: The Falk Clan Series Boxed Set Books 1-4

Dragon Mates 2: The Falk Clan Series Boxed Set Books

<u>The Bear Claw Tales:</u>

Bearly Breathing: A Bear Claw Tale 1

Bearly There: A Bear Claw Tale 2

Bearly Tamed: A Bear Claw Tale 3

Bearly Mated: A Bear Claw Tale 4

Also available in a boxed set:

The Complete Bear Claw Tales (Books 1-4)

<u>The Barvale Clan Tales:</u>

Polar Opposites: The Barvale Clan Tales 1

Polar Outbreak: The Barvale Clan Tales 2

Polar Compound: A Barvale Clan Tale 3

Polar Curve: A Barvale Clan Tale 4

Also available in a boxed set:

The Barvale Clan Tales (Books 1-4)

<u>Barvale Holiday Tales:</u>

A Bear For Christmas

Hers To Bear

Thank You Beary Much

Bearing Gifts

Also available in a boxed set:

The Barvale Holiday Tales (Books 1-3)

Purely Paranormal Romance Books:

Marked by the Devil: Purely Paranormal Romance Books

Mated to the Dragon King: Purely Paranormal Romance Books

Claimed by the Demon: Purely Paranormal Romance Books

Christmas with a Devil, a Dragon King, & a Demon: Purely Paranormal Romance Books

Vampire Lover: Purely Paranormal Romance Books

Grizzly Lover: Purely Paranormal Romance Books

Christmas With Her Chupacabra: Purely Paranormal Romance Books

Purely Paranormal Romance Books Anthology

The Wardens of Terra:

Bound by Air: The Wardens of Terra Book 1

Star Kissed: A Wardens of Terra Short

Waterlocked: The Wardens of Terra Book 2

Moon Kissed: A Wardens of Terra Short

*Now in a boxed set and in audio!

The Maverick Pride Tales:

Purrfectly Mated

Purrfectly Kissed

Purrfectly Trapped

Purrfectly Caught

Purrfectly Naughty

Purrfectly Bound

Purrfectly Paired

<u>Dire Wolf Mates:</u>

Shake That Sass

Breaking Sass

Pinch of Sass

Kickin' Sass

<u>Wyvern Protection Unit:</u>

Gift Wrapped Protector: WPU 1

<u>Standalones:</u>

The Enforcer

Blood Song: A Sanguinem Council Book

Spring Fling (co-written with P. Mattern)

<u>EveL Worlds:</u>

Chinchilla and the Devil: A FUCN'A Book

Sammi and the Jersey Bull: A FUCN'A Book

Mouse and the Ball: A FUCN'A Book

Chicken and the Paparazzi: A FUCN'A Book

Jersey Sure Shifters Books 1-3 anthology

<u>The Guardians of Chaos:</u>

Wolf Shield: Guardians of Chaos Book 1

Dragon Shield: Guardians of Chaos Book 2

Stallion Shield: Guardians of Chaos Book 3

Panther Shield: Guardians of Chaos 4

Witch Shield: Guardians of Chaos 5

Vampire Shield: Guardians of Chaos 6

Guardians of Chaos Volume 1 Books 1-3

Guardians of Chaos Volume 2 Books 4-6

Howl's Romance

Mated to the Werewolf Next Door: A Howl's Romance

The Tiger King's Christmas Bride

Claiming His Virgin Mate: Howls Romance

Twice Mated Tales

Doubly Claimed

Doubly Bound

Doubly Tied

Twice Mated Tales Anthology

Hearts of Stone Series

Shifter Mountain: Hearts of Stone 1

Shifter City: Hearts of Stone 2

Shifter Village: Hearts of Stone 3

Hearts of Stone Books 1-3 Anthology

<u>Accidentally Undead Series</u>

Fangs For Nothin'

<u>Moongate Island Tales</u>

Moongate Island Mate

Moongate Island Christmas Claim

<u>Mated in Hope Falls</u>

Mated by Moonlight

<u>Speed Dating with the Denizens of the Underworld</u>

Ash: Speed Dating with the Denizens of Underworld

Arachne: Speed Dating with the Denizens of Underworld

Asterion: Speed Dating with the Denizens of Underworld

<u>Hungry Fur Love</u>

Hungry Like Her Wolf: Magic and Mayhem Universe

Hungry For Her Bear: Magic and Mayhem Universe

<u>Shifters Unleashed Boxed Sets</u>

<u>Island Stripe Pride</u>

Tiger Claimed

Tiger Denied

Tiger Rejected

*Tiger Tales Anthology

<u>NYC Shifter Tales</u>

Cuff Linked

Sealed Fate

<u>A Howlin' Good Fairytale Retelling</u>

Sweet As Candy (single edition coming soon)

<u>Coming Soon:</u>

Hungry As Her Python: Magic and Mayhem Universe

Bearly Friends

If The Shoe Fits: A Howlin' Good Fairytale Retelling

The Wolf's Winter Wish: A Macconwood Pack Tale

The Hybrid Assassin

For Fangs Sake

Tempted By Her Protector: WPU 2

Alien Protector: WPU 3

Unexpected Protector: WPU 4

Thrilled By Her Protector: WPU 5

###

<u>Young Adult Urban Fantasy Books:</u>

Wolf Moon: A Grazi Kelly Novel Book 1

Hunter Moon: A Grazi Kelly Novel Book 2

Rebel Moon: A Grazi Kelly Novel Book 3

Winter Moon: A Grazi Kelly Novel Book 4

Chasing The Moon: A Grazi Kelly Short 5

Blood Moon: A Grazi Kelly Novel 6

*Get all 6 books NOW AVAILABLE IN A BOXED SET:

The Complete Grazi Kelly Novel Series

Casting Magic: The Angela Tanner Files 1

Keeping Magic: The Angela Tanner Files 2

<u>G'Witches Magical Mysteries Series</u>

Co-written with P. Mattern

G'Witches

G'Witches 2: The Harpy Harbinger

G'Witches 3: Summoning Secrets

EXCERPT FROM PURRFECTLY MATED

How the fuck did I wind up here?

It was all Elissa could do not to slam her face down on the table as she pondered that question for the umpteenth time since leaving her cozy Hoboken apartment to go on this so called date.

"So, babe," the over-stuffed, heavily-cologned, and downright fugly man said.

Her date of the evening looked like something out of a bad sitcom as he tried to lean over the stained tablecloth of the rundown hotel buffet room, he'd driven two hours to get to. Waggling his caterpillar-like eyebrows, he gave her the once over and Elissa's skin crawled.

Oh, hell no.

"I got a room upstairs, you know, for *after*," he told her, nodding his head, and biting his lower lip in a manner she assumed he thought was provocative.

At best, it was nauseating.

FML.

How was this guy Elissa's date for the evening? What had she done to deserve this?

Little Gianni. Yup, that was how he'd introduced himself. And here she was. On a blind date with a guy who had the word 'little' in front of his name.

Well, what did she expect? Roses and champagne? In this economy? She didn't know where Cinder-fucking-ella got her prince, but it sure as fuck wasn't in Jersey.

Elissa could only blame herself for agreeing to go on this blind date. Initially, the whole Little Gianni fiasco had been intended for her roommate.

Wait a second. Scratch that thought.

It *was* all Gretchen's fault. That ungrateful cow!

She tried to play it off like she was some sweet little homegrown maiden. Oh, just wait till Elissa got home. Gretchen was never going to hear the end of it.

She owed Elissa. Big time. Like a whole month of

washing the dishes big time. The rat trap they shared in her hometown of Hoboken was all the two women could afford, and for the most part, they got along just fine.

In fact, they'd grown to be close friends over the three years they'd lived together. It was the only reason she'd ever agreed to this date from Hell.

Elissa sighed and looked over at Little Gianni. Maybe he wasn't all that bad?

"*BEEEELLLLLLLLCHHH!* 'Scuse me, doll. Better out, am I right?"

Gianni winked and Elissa wished for a black hole to open up and swallow her up right through the floor.

OMFG.

The man just burped out loud like he was in a frat boy belting contest, only those days passed him up about thirty years ago.

For fuck's sake. Gretchen, you so owe me.

Elissa cursed her roommate and tried not to groan. But Little Gianni wasn't quite done. The grown ass man lifted his leg and let one rip.

Right. Fucking. There.

Elissa was going to die before the end of the night.

Literally.

This is what you get when you do a friend a favor without asking for details! Idiota!

The voice of her Italian grandmother sounded in her brain. She tried to ignore it, willing herself not to wince at the man while he sucked air, and who knows what else, noisily through his coffee-stained teeth.

Ew. So gross.

That was the perfect word to describe it. The only word, in fact. The entire date was just so fucking gross. She still couldn't believe her sweet little roommate from Iowa, *Gretchen Kaepernick*, she of the wispy hair and baby blues, had set her up with this guy!

What the actual fuck was up with that?

Little Gianni was a slob. Actually, he looked just like her Uncle Nico, and that was not a good thing. Seriously, not good at all.

He wore his hair slicked back in a too tight ponytail that emphasized his rapidly receding hairline. As if that wasn't enough to put her off, he was sporting an enormous paunch. Now, being a curvy girl, Elissa appreciated food and was in no way against men showing the same appreciation.

She liked bigger men. Always had. But bigger did not mean you had to be sloppy. Little Gianni's stomach was literally hanging out from under a tight tan golf shirt that had definitely seen better days.

The man didn't even look like he had ever played a sport of any kind. With it, he wore brown polyester pants that were three inches above his ankles and unbuttoned at the waist.

He didn't look like he tried at all for this date. What kind of guy did that? His shirt collar was bent and wrinkled, and all three buttons were open to his chest, revealing a mat of oily, dark hair and pimples.

Somehow, he'd managed to tuck the back of the shirt in, but the front simply would not hold in that stomach. What worried her more were the tight brown pants.

As he sat back and stretched, she wondered if she should take cover. They looked like they were one bite from exploding off his body. Elissa shuddered at the image.

Please God, if You have an ounce of mercy, don't let that happen, she prayed.

"Hang on, doll, I gotta take this," he said, and turned to answer his cell phone.

It was ringing to the tune of '70s disco music she

hadn't heard since the last family reunion. Her eyes kept going to the huge stain on the front of his shirt. It was a little game she liked to call *what the hell is that*.

Coffee, she guessed.

"Up your ass, Bruno. I gotta have it by Monday," he cursed into the receiver.

Elissa winced at the spectacle he was making of them both. There were only a handful of people there, but still.

Deep breaths.

Ew. Maybe not.

She coughed as the strong body spray, that he'd obviously used a ton of in lieu of a shower, bad move in her opinion, invaded her lungs.

Oh, this was so bad.

Elissa was, by no means, a snob. But this guy looked like he'd stepped out of a bad 1980s mafia spoof film. What's worse, he kept smacking his lips together as he hung up the phone and looked her over from head to chest.

Thank fuck for the table, she thought, wishing she could hide her bosoms from his view.

"Ssssss," he hissed, like it was sexy or something.

She just grimaced. Elissa might be able to forgive a lot of quirks, but she hated mouth noises. Really hated them. It was a super pet peeve of hers. Never mind his totally inappropriate and unwelcomed leer.

She started counting the minutes, willing the date to be over already. Plenty of people would tell her she shouldn't be so choosy, but really? She was not this desperate.

Not yet anyway.

So, she was curvy and a little mouthy too. But was it wrong to want a man with good table manners? Even if men were thin on the ground for someone like her.

As a chef, she'd worked in a lot of restaurants and even as a personal cook for professional couples. She'd seen her fair share of unhappy couples and downright uncomfortable marriages. But as far as she was concerned, all relationships went downhill when good table manners were dismissed.

Good manners were merely a sign that a person was thoughtful and respectful. At least, that was what Nonna had told her. Gianni here had clearly missed that lesson as a child. Elissa had to work not to groan in disgust as he slurped a raw clam down his gullet.

Shudder.

Was there no end to his feeding? That's what it reminded her of. Feeding time at the zoo.

OMG. That was rude, she scolded herself. But it wasn't like she said it out loud.

All she wanted to do was go home. At least she was comfortable. *She'd* worn her softest pair of black leggings for this disaster date, paired with one of her favorite tunics on top.

It was dark green with tiny black buttons down the front and showed just the right amount of cleavage. She'd gone for neat and tidy as opposed to downright sexy.

Good call, in her opinion. Elissa looked perfectly fine for a nice *getting to know you* dinner, which is what she thought she was getting when her roommate asked her to step in for her on a blind date that one of her best client's had set up for her.

Elissa shuddered now, thinking how good old Gianni here would've reacted to the red dress and heels she'd contemplated before checking the weather report.

Gulp.

The lewd man was already salivating, and she was so not having it. Fending off his unwanted advances was not how she wanted to finish the night.

Ew again.

Elissa shivered, slightly chilled despite the fact

they were indoors. It was a cold, gloomy evening, and the forecast called for even more rain later that night. Not at all unusual for this time of year in the Garden State.

November was always chilly in the evenings, rainy too. Elissa tended to run warm, but she was glad she'd brought a jacket with her. Especially since her date refused to turn the heat on in the car.

When she'd asked, he'd looked offended and told her it wasted gas.

Um. Okay.

She checked her phone. It was only seven o'clock, but the two hour drive was still ahead of them. Maybe they could make it home before ten if they left soon.

Ugh. Did he just blow his nose?

"Allergies, doll. Say, you gonna eat that?" he asked before scooping a fry from her dish and swallowing it down.

Elissa was gonna kill her roomie. Gretchen was a hair and nail stylist. A lot of her clients were elderly, and they just loved her. They were always offering to set her up on blind dates with their nephews and grandsons.

Mostly, the sweet old ladies were kind. They swore they could find her curvy roommate the right man, assuming she was single because she was new to town. Well, when Elissa got home tonight, she was going to tell Gretchen she needed to fire the old lady who set this date up from being her client.

Like *ASAP*.

No one who liked Gretchen would've sent her out with this guy. Gianni reached over and touched her hand and Elissa pulled back, reaching for the napkin.

Gross.

"I sure hope you ain't a cold one, doll," he said, shaking his head.

"What?"

"Ain't gonna matter. I know just what you need, doll."

She was still wiping the greasy residue he'd transferred to her skin from the food he ate sans utensils. This was too much. Elissa was beyond uncomfortable with all the leering and bad attempts at innuendo.

Plus, she was starving. One look at the dump he'd taken her to, and she knew she could never eat there. The chef in her wouldn't allow it.

To think they drove two hours for this! She'd practically frozen to death in his maroon Cadillac, listening to a CD of the Rat Pack, while Gianni crooned loudly, and off key, to the music.

Normally, she was a fan of the famous group of legendary singers. Having grown up in Hoboken, she couldn't not be a Sinatra fan. Though, to be honest, Dean Martin had always been her favorite.

Still, Elissa was a firm believer that there were just some people you did not try to imitate. Especially not if you were Little Gianni. While he was belting his heart out, he'd been trying to get his right hand on her thigh. She'd asked him politely to stop.

Twice.

Then she'd been forced to try something a little more drastic. Like spilling her hot tea on the offending hand the third time he'd tried it. Finally, he'd removed his hand from her leg. Not making a fourth attempt, which she was grateful for.

Elissa should've taken that behavior as a sign and gotten out of the car. But no. She'd wanted to do Gretchen a solid. So, against her better judgement, she gave the creep another chance.

Idiota, her grandmother's voice echoed in her brain again.

The old woman had loved her. Elissa knew that without a doubt. She'd raised her after her own

parents had passed on in a tragic automobile accident when Elissa was just twelve.

Her grandmother was a no-nonsense kind of
lady who dished out priceless wisdom with brutally
honest insights. It was the same way she dished out
huge bowls of pasta with her amazing meatballs and
homemade sauce. Not to mention a side order of
back-breaking hugs that Elissa still missed.

Nonna cooked like that all the time. She made a
huge pot of sauce every weekend, and she was happy
to serve it to Elissa and her teammates and friends,
especially after games and tournaments.

Soccer had been her sport of choice, and cooking
had soon become her favorite hobby. Her grandmother had encouraged her in both pursuits.
Guiding her in one and cheering her on in the other.
Elissa still missed her terribly.

"Hey babe, ain't you gonna eat nothin'? You know
they charge twenty dollars just to sit down," Little
Gianni interrupted her train of thought.

Elissa was forced to turn her mind back to the
present, which unfortunately included watching, *and
hearing*, him as he sucked on his teeth and stuffed
another breaded shrimp down his throat.

"I'm fine," she answered with a polite smile plas-
tered on her face.

Just get home, Lissa. Just get him to take you home.

Elissa closed her eyes when he looked back down at his dish. Thank God for small favors, she mused. At least he was more interested in eating at the moment.

He'd taken her to the rattiest looking hotel and casino she'd ever seen in her life. And the buffet room?

Ew.

Seriously, the place had to be violating at least a dozen health codes. When Gianni had said Atlantic City, she'd thought at least the atmosphere would be exciting. But they were so far from the real glitz and entertainment, they might as well be anywhere else.

She sighed, looking at the plate she'd made for herself. Elissa couldn't even fake an interest in the food. As a chef, it was hard enough to dine out.

She was always judging the food, the service, the ingredients. How could she not? It was her business. And that was when the food was good!

This was not good. Not at all.

She'd been to hospitals that served better food. Old yellow lights buzzed and blinked around the buffet, giving it an abandoned kind of feel. The menu was made up of mostly frozen then fried or baked cuisine.

Reheated actually. It was like a giant TV dinner buffet where every item was previously frozen when already cooked and warmed up in an oven.

It was the kind of food sold cheap at restaurant supply stores in bulk. Yeah, this was much worse than hospital food, in her opinion.

There was a worn carpet on the floor, a handful of scattered tables in the dining room, elevator music on in the background, and the entire place smelled like canned soup.

Not to mention not one of the five people there besides them was under sixty years old.

"Gianni," she said, leaning forward so as not to hurt his feelings.

"I thought you mentioned something about seeing a show tonight. Is it here?"

Please don't be here.

If he was taking her somewhere else, she could beg off and hire a cab to take her home. There was no way she was sitting through anything else with this man. Not now. Not ever.

"Ah, I see, babe, you want some entertainment first, I get it," he snickered loudly, and she blanched.

Whatever he thought was going to happen wasn't. She needed to disabuse him of the notion, and fast.

"Alright, alright. Lemme finish this, babe. Then we'll go up to the room I got for us," he said.

Before she could make sense of the ludicrous statement, he slurped another fried shrimp, don't ask how. Then he grabbed her arm and yanked her from the seat before she could even react.

Elissa tugged on his hold, but the man was immovable. Tossing a five-dollar bill on the table, Little Gianni snatched a toothpick from the hostess stand before dragging her outside.

Great, he was a cheap tipper, too.

All she wanted was to go home. Figuring the best way to do that would probably be to get him to the car, she let him lead the way.

Once inside, she would ask him to drive back to Hoboken so she could wring Gretchen's neck. Fuming, she pulled her arm out of his hand and walked behind him.

The rain was really pouring, and the cheap bastard had refused valet. Elissa ducked her head so she wouldn't get so wet. Of course, the jacket she'd brought was light and had no hood.

Gianni had an umbrella, but he didn't offer to hold it for her, and honestly, she did not relish the idea of getting any closer to him than necessary.

Seriously, not happening.

Now all she had to do was break the news. She had no intention of watching a show or returning to the hotel with him.

What could go wrong?

Grab your copy at https://www.cdgorri.com/books/purrfectly-mated!

EXCERPT FROM BOUND BY AIR

Troy Waman looked down at his smartphone to the little red arrow blinking on his map app, indicating he had reached his destination. He frowned pensively before shaking his head.

"What a fucking shithole," he murmured to himself as he exited the nondescript black SUV his Station Master, Rex, had given him for the job.

"*Try not to scratch it,*" the tough Bear shifter had said with a barely contained growl after their meeting the day before last. After a thousand years of waiting, The *Wardens of Terra* were being called to duty and this was Troy's first assignment.

It took him a day and a half to make his way to Shadowland, New York from the little suburb in Virginia Beach where his Station was located. There

233

were dozens of them across the continental United States and even more overseas, though he'd rarely been out of the county himself.

Troy rolled his shoulders and exhaled. He was the first from his Station to be called to duty. A fact that left him both proud and humbled at the same time. He'd trained damn hard since he was a child waiting for such an opportunity. Now he had it, and it was almost too much to bear.

Fuck and damn. It's time Troy, get your ass in gear. That was all the sympathy he had for himself. Why the hell should he have any at all? Troy Waman was no tenderfoot normal. He was a Warden of Terra. He didn't need to remind himself of the honor and duty that went along with his position.

The *Wardens of Terra* were an ancient group of elite warriors. All of them Shifters. Identified in their youth and trained throughout their preternaturally long lives, they were guardians as well as fighters. *Station Masters* led teams of Wardens across the planet.

Though they'd been deactivated sometime in the last millennium, Wardens were born, chosen, and trained every day with the distinct knowledge that someday, they'd be called upon to defend the earth. That day was here.

Troy Waman had been trained as a Warden since before he learned how to spell the word. His heritage was a mix of Anglo and Native American. His father's blood was a mix of tribes including Algonquin, Lenape, Cherokee, and a few others. He hadn't stuck around long enough for anyone to learn the rest.

He supposed he could get a DNA test, but that might raise too many questions with the normals. Especially in this day of advanced technology in biogenetics.

Besides, it was quite common in today's world to find Native American peoples descended from multiple tribes. Troy Waman was uncommon for an entirely different reason. He was a Shifter, a special race of dual natured beings with one foot in the supernatural world and one in the human. Troy was a *Thunderbird Shifter* to be exact. Something unique even amongst Shifters.

He stretched his long, lithe body as he stepped away from the vehicle. It was already dark out despite it being fairly early in the evening. *Daylight savings my ass.* He sniffed the frigid air. The unusually high winds made the cold seem even more bitter. The street lamp stuttered on the corner, a rusty fence squeaked, and a black cat crossed the street, ducking under some parked cars. Troy's frown deepened.

It looked like the setting of a B-horror flick. All it needed was some half naked co-ed to run down the street with a masked bogeyman stalking behind her, traditional blood-coated knife in hand. *Oh yeah.* They might call it *Shadowland Nightmare* or something equally cheesy.

He stopped his musings and used his heightened senses to take in the downtrodden area around him. It would seem upstate New York wasn't all orchards and sprawling suburbs. He smirked as the "I love New York" song ran through his head. *Yeah, right.*

Apparently, parts of the Empire State were as fucked up as the street where he was born in Newark, New Jersey. He'd visited that shithole back when he was in his teens just out of curiosity. What a mistake that had been! He'd left almost as soon as he'd arrived. His extended family had been, shall we say, less than welcoming.

His gray-haired grandmother had screamed and crossed herself when he stepped over her threshold. He was what they called a *skin walker*. They feared and loathed him as something evil. Him evil? Like he was the motherfucker who knocked-up some unsuspecting normal and left her ass with a Shifter baby.

He was not evil, but he was something they did not understand. He'd been angry and ashamed that day. He'd crashed through his grandmother's kitchen to hitch a ride back down to his Station in Virginia Beach.

In his youth it was more like a military training camp, but it was all he knew of home. After all, it was where he'd lived his entire life. He'd made his peace and settled fully into his life there.

The incident with his grandmother had happened over a decade ago, when Troy had stolen his records out of Rex's office. Still, the memory remained fresh in his mind as if it were only yesterday. The fucked-up street where he was standing only brought back the painful reminder that he'd come from the same kind of squalor. *Fuck this*, he thought.

The pungent scent of despair washed over him. *Reminding him.* A young man with a hood pulled up over his head, eyed him from the street corner. *Drug dealer. Shadowland* indeed. It was an apt name for this shamble of a neighborhood.

The young man continued to stare until Troy allowed his beast to shine through. His golden eyes pinned the errant youth through the inky darkness of the night. Startled, the kid dropped the bag he was holding and ran down the alley.

Punk. Troy walked over and picked up what he had so hastily left behind. A couple of grams of crack cocaine and heroin, *probably cut with Fentanyl.* There were also various sized baggies full of what smelled like some below average marijuana and half-rotted psychedelic mushrooms.

Just your garden variety of illegal substances to be found on most street corners in neighborhoods like this one. *Fucking normals.* He frowned and dumped the still sealed contents down the closest storm drain. He sent a quick text to Rex earmarking the location.

Rex would make sure the local police department got an anonymous tip to retrieve the narcotics before someone got hurt. Recreational drug use, mainly the opioid epidemic, was wreaking havoc amongst the humans with more and more of them succumbing to their addictions.

It was troubling, but not Troy's problem. Shifters were extraordinarily hard to kill. Most human drugs had little to no effect on supernatural beings. *Normals,* he growled the thought, *such weak creatures.*

To be fair, Shifters had vices too. He just had little

experience with it. Cecil, a Station-mate of his, had an adrenaline addiction. He was always putting himself in dangerous situations, even during simple training exercises. Fernandez, a Jaguar Shifter, was always trying to get into some chick's pants. *Sex addict.* And he knew of others who channeled their energies into ways he considered to be mostly unproductive.

His opinion, for sure. He'd always been something of a loner by nature. There weren't many Thunderbird Shifters around. Hell, he was the only fucking one he knew of in this part of the world.

He didn't blame or judge his Station-mates for their proclivities. Most of the Shifters he knew had large appetites which included food, exercise, and sex.

Troy had certainly explored that part of him. He wasn't a man-whore or anything, but he'd had his share of women. None of them mattered to him. Just a means to satisfy the occasional itch.

Troy was determined to live his life as a Warden of Terra alone. He never expected to find anyone willing to share what was a potentially deadly existence.

Those who followed the Darkness and evil were always looking for ways to gain the upper hand and it was his job to stop them. The way he saw it, it was an honor and a duty to serve.

He shared this great responsibility with the entire organization. The core belief of the Wardens was based on one indisputable fact Shifters had walked the earth since the dawn of time, even before humankind; therefore, they were responsible for the well-being of the entire planet and all its inhabitants. Especially those who were inherently weaker. Mainly females and *normals*.

There were other supernaturals who believed humans, or normals as they referred to them, were a blight on the planet. Those creatures wished to destroy them and take over.

Demons, Dark Witches, and a whole plethora of evil beings sought the destruction of the normals and the world they lived in. *Idiots! Did they even realize if they destroyed the world, there would be nothing left? Where the fuck would they live?*

Of course, the supernatural world had many agencies that worked towards the common goal of saving the planet. The *Order of the Guardians,* for example, were responsible for policing the various factions of supernaturals.

Shifters generally tended to ally themselves with the Guardians. Sure, there were *bad* Shifters, but he'd never come across any willing to follow the Dark. Simply because most agreed the destruction of the world could not be allowed to happen.

Different Packs and Clans, etcetera, of course, had different ideas. Some wanted to remain secret, others wished to come out, and other still wanted to rule the weaker humans. It was a whole fucking thing, and they argued about regularly.

Troy didn't know from any of that. He spent little time in the human world. His efforts better spent making himself worthy of being a Warden. Training, exercise, and following orders. That's what Troy lived for, it was why he was chosen.

Thunderbird Shifters were very rare. *Special.* He scoffed at the stray thought. But no matter what way he looked at it, Troy was indeed unique. In more ways than one. He was born *marked* by the stars. A *Shifter of Terra.*

From infancy, he was told he carried the power of his sign within him. *Aquarius* ruled his destiny and it would aid him in the never-ending battle against the forces of darkness.

Every single Warden he knew was a Shifter like him. They were the fiercest warriors on the planet. Like many others throughout the last thousand years, Troy, *a Shifter child who was marked,* was taken from his parents and trained by his Station Master until the time when he would be called into use.

All that time, he thought, *and here I am.* He tried to ignore the pressure building inside of him. He felt anxious. His animal pressed against his psyche, comforting him with his presence.

The significance of the moment was not lost on him. The Wardens had waited a millennium to be called to act. *He* had been waiting his entire life.

"Do not fear the future, Troy," the Herald who had visited his Station said to him when he'd brought word that they had been activated, *"Your destiny awaits."*

Troy wondered if the old man referred to the Wardens finally being called to act, or if the elder spoke of yet another legend. Troy had been shocked to say the least when the Herald had entered their tidy little Station in Virginia Beach with his flowing white hair. After he told them the news, he turned to Troy and recited another old tale.

"Young Thunderbird, you are the first to return us to Terra. Do not doubt your worth. Your destiny has been written in the stars since before you were born, Troy Waman. Remember, a Warden discovers his true measure when his fated mate is thrust upon him."

Whatever the fuck that meant. Troy looked down at

his phone, then to the street sign on the corner, and finally, to the faded numbers painted on the mailbox in front of the ramble of a house his map app had brought him to.

Fuck, am I thinking? Fated mates are myths. Stories made up so orphaned Shifters would sleep through the night. He scoffed at the thought. Memories of tales the head nurse, Sr. Maria, had told him at the training camp he'd called home for years invaded his brain.

Memories were pesky things. Sometimes eternal, and always fucking portable. But he was no longer a child. *No more stories, Sister. Now, I act.*

"A thousand years we've waited, and I'm walking into a fucking scene from a bad episode of *Hoarders,*" Troy shook his head and frowned at the decrepit house that sat a few hundred feet away from him.

It was cold as fuck outside and his leather jacket did little to warm him. Avian Shifters did not carry around the same bulk as other types of Shifters. He ran hotter than normals, but the single digit temperature froze him to the bone.

True, he wasn't beefy like some of his fellow Shifters, but he was just as incredibly strong, and he was wicked fast. Much stronger than any average male. He paused briefly gauging the atmosphere.

There was something off about the place. He scented *Magic* and something else. His Bird bristled beneath his skin. *Easy now.*

Lightning flashed in the darkened skies, allowing him to see the worn shingles, and cracked siding of the beaten-up colonial in greater detail. More than one window had been smashed and boarded up with cheap plywood.

If anything, it enhanced the creepy haunted house feel of the place. The porch sagged danger-ously. He wondered how the place had managed to not be condemned by the town. One thing was certain, it was an ugly little turd of a house.

Who the hell put gray siding on their house anyway? Maybe it wasn't always that color. Maybe the owner liked gray. *Whatever.* He couldn't give two shits about the siding.

His only concern was the increased supernatural activity in the area over the past two weeks. Ever since the owner, a *Mrs. Renalda Curosi,* passed away. *A haunting?*

A creaking sound floated up to his ears and he stilled his movements. The sound developed into more of a *moaning* noise. An unearthly wail. It grew louder as the lightning continued to flash in the sky.

Troy had never seen a ghost. True, there were a

lot of things in the universe he had never seen nor heard of, but that didn't make them any less real.

If ghosts were real, and they made noises, he imagined that pitiful wail was damn close to what it would sound like.

No such thing as ghosts. Yeah, well, most people had never heard of Shifters either. And yet, there he stood.

His Thunderbird shifted once more beneath his skin, the beast flexing his senses as the lightning in the air drew him to the surface. *No.* He told his other half. His human needed to be in control now. He walked across the street, keeping to the shadows.

Something was indeed off about the creepy old house. He inched further to the black door. The knocker was in the shape of a face or mask. No discernible features, just a vague impression of eyes, nose, and mouth. *Shadowland indeed.*

He listened with his enhanced hearing and frowned. There was a distinct voice somewhere beneath the moaning and creaking. A *female* voice. His curiosity was piqued.

From what he'd seen in her file, Mrs. Curosi was ninety-seven when she passed. Her closest living relative was a half-sister, a *Magdelena Kristos*, and she lived over three hours away in New Jersey. The half-sister was cut from Mrs. Curosi's will recently. She'd bequeathed her entire estate, house, bank account, and all her earthly belongings, to someone named *A. Kristos. Another sister? Maybe.*

Troy hadn't given it much thought until now. A crash sounded from inside the house. He perked up as the feminine voice he'd thought he'd heard earlier screamed in pain. *Time to act.*

Grab your copy at https://www.cdgorri.com/books/bound-by-airbooks/bound-by-air!

About the Author

C.D. Gorri is a USA Today Bestselling author of steamy paranormal romance and urban fantasy. She is the creator of the Grazi Kelly Universe.

Join her mailing list here: https://www.cdgorri.com/newsletter

An avid reader with a profound love for books and literature, when she is not writing or taking care of her family, she can usually be found with a book or tablet in hand. C.D. lives in her home state of New Jersey where many of her characters or stories are based. Her tales are fast paced yet detailed with satisfying conclusions.

If you enjoy powerful heroines and loyal heroes who face relatable problems in supernatural settings, journey into the Grazi Kelly Universe today. You will find sassy, curvy heroines and sexy, love-driven heroes who find their HEAs between the pages. Werewolves, Bears, Dragons, Tigers, Witches, Romani, Lynxes, Foxes, Thunderbirds, Vampires, and many more Shifters and supernatural creatures dwell within her worlds. The most important thing is every mate in this universe is fated, loyal, and true lovers always get their happily ever afters.

Want to know how it all began? Enter the Grazi Kelly Universe with Wolf Moon: A Grazi Kelly Novel or pick up Charley's Christmas Wolf and dive into the Macconwood Pack Novel Series today.

For a complete list of C.D. Gorri's books visit her website here:

https://www.cdgorri.com/complete-book-list/

Thank you and happy reading!

del mare alla stella,
    C.D. Gorri

Follow C.D. Gorri here:
    http://www.cdgorri.com
    https://www.facebook.com/Cdgorribooks

https://www.bookbub.com/authors/c-d-gorri
https://twitter.com/cgor22
https://instagram.com/cdgorri/
https://www.goodreads.com/cdgorri
https://www.tiktok.com/@cdgorriauthor

www.ingramcontent.com/pod-product-compliance
Lightning Source LLC
Chambersburg PA
CBHW061234210726
48293CB00003B/760